*Thanis smiled. 'I knew y . . . .
beginning, but I had to make sure. Jessica, I have a commission
for you.'*

It is the chance of a lifetime, the lucky break that Jessica has
always dreamed of, an opportunity to really make her name
as an artist. It is only when Jessica arrives at the isolated
house in Cornwall with the mysterious and enigmatic
Thanis that she begins to have doubts. Why is the silver
spiral that Jessica is to make so vital to Thanis? Why is
Thanis so keen to keep Jessica away from her friends and
her past life? And why are there so many cats around?

As she becomes engrossed in making the spiral, Jessica has
no time to wonder whether there will be a price to pay for her
success—and whether the price will be more than she could
ever have imagined.

HAZEL RILEY was born in Gateshead and discovered a passion for
reading as a child. That's when she decided she was going to be a
writer. She studied English Literature at York University, becoming a
Trotskyist, a radical feminist, and a Buddhist in rapid succession.
After university she moved to London, did a variety of jobs, and spent
some time in Egypt, developing a love of all things Egyptian. She now
lives in London with her dog and divides her time between teaching
adult literacy and writing for children. *Thanis* is her first novel for
Oxford University Press.

Thanis

Thanis

Hazel Riley

OXFORD
UNIVERSITY PRESS

OXFORD

UNIVERSITY PRESS

Great Clarendon Street, Oxford OX2 6DP

Oxford University Press is a department of the University of Oxford.
It furthers the University's objective of excellence in research, scholarship,
and education by publishing worldwide in

Oxford New York

Athens Auckland Bangkok Bogotá Beunos Aires Calcutta
Cape Town Chennai Dar es Salaam Delhi Florence Hong Kong Istanbul
Karachi Kuala Lumpur Madrid Melbourne Mexico City Mumbai
Nairobi Paris São Paulo Singapore Taipei Tokyo Toronto Warsaw

with associated companies in Berlin Ibadan

Oxford is a registered trade mark of Oxford University Press
in the UK and in certain other countries

British Library Cataloguing in Publication Data available

ISBN 0 19 271831 2

Typeset by AFS Image Setters Ltd, Glasgow
Printed in Great Britain

For Rosemary, who has her own
powers of regeneration

1

I'm plagued by one thought. Am I responsible for everything that happened? It's with me night and day. I can't escape it. The fear. It even haunts my dreams.

I'm haunted by Thanis too. I can't forget her. She's engraved in my memory along with all the strange things that happened that summer. I see her lurking in the shadows. I hear her voice carried on the wind. I feel her presence, watching me. I'll never be free of her.

I know I'm not crazy. You see, before I met her I was very ordinary. I had a room in an ordinary house in Camden Town, went to an ordinary college, just wanted the ordinary things out of life: to be a success, make money, enjoy myself. There was nothing special about me. I've got a couple of GCSEs and was never expected to achieve much. I come from an averagely unhappy family. My parents divorced when I was 10. I left home as soon as I could after one row too many with my mother.

I was always so down to earth. I never had nightmares. I wasn't afraid of the dark. I didn't believe in ghosts or witches, didn't like horror movies and had never had my fortune told. That was before I met Thanis. Was it really only a year ago? It feels like an age.

It's a difficult story to tell. I don't understand it myself yet. Maybe I never will. I don't know how it will finish, or if I'll live long enough to find out. You won't believe me, but I must try. I can't keep it to myself any longer.

It's not hard to know where to start. It all began that afternoon in the museum. I'd been living in London for

1

about six months and I was enjoying my independence. I was working on a project for my GNVQ Art and Design and I'd gone to the museum to sketch. I was sitting in the Egyptian Sculpture Gallery, trying to draw the statue of a lion goddess. I couldn't get the head right. I was concentrating hard when a movement in the distance caught my eye. I looked up. I saw someone stumble in the doorway, framed by two sphinxes that sat in glass cases at either side of the entrance. It was a woman, but I couldn't see her face because it was curtained by her long, dark hair. She seemed to be having trouble getting up again. No one else was near so I went to help her.

'It is nothing. I will be stronger in a minute,' she said as I helped her limp to a seat. 'I must have slipped on something.' She looked very pale, like someone who has been ill for a long time.

'I'll go and get help,' I said. I could see a guard across the room. Her hand shot out and grabbed my wrist. I was surprised at how strong her grip was.

'No. Please don't bother. It will pass in a minute.'

'I'll go back to my drawing, then,' I said, 'if you're sure you're OK.'

'Your drawing?'

'Yes. I'm an art student.'

'Here, let me see.'

I didn't want to show her, but as she reached out for the pad I found myself handing it over to her.

'It is not so bad,' she said, 'just change this line here.' She traced the side of the face with her finger.

I could see what she meant immediately. I got my pen and did as she suggested. Suddenly the drawing seemed to spring into life. It was much better than I'd thought. It had a strange energy. Funny what a difference seeing it through someone else's eyes can make, I thought.

I left her resting. I went back to my work with a new confidence. The next time I looked up she had gone. That was when I saw it. It was lying in the shadow of the sphinxes where she had stumbled, right in my line of vision. I was sure it was hers, I don't know why. I couldn't see it properly from that distance so I went over and picked it up. It was about the size of a little finger nail, gold I think. It looked like a letter, but not from any alphabet I knew. Maybe it was a good luck charm. It felt vaguely warm on my palm.

Whatever it was, I slipped it into my pocket and went back to my drawing. I meant to hand it in on my way out, but when I got to the information desk I couldn't find it. When I got home I found it in my bag. I put it in a drawer and soon forgot about it. It was some weeks later when she rang.

2

It was very late. I'd just caught a night bus back from Soho where I'd been with Jim, who I'd just started going out with. I picked up the receiver warily. At first no one spoke and I wondered if it was a crank call. I was about to hang up when a strange voice said, 'Jessica.' I couldn't think who it was.

'Yes. Who is this?' I answered.

'I met you at the museum. You gave them your number. I believe you found the rune.' She spoke slowly, pronouncing each word carefully.

'The what?' I still had no idea who she was. To be honest, I was a bit suspicious. You have to be cautious these days. It was after midnight. I think the friends I share with were in, but they were probably in bed. Then it suddenly clicked who she was. 'Oh, the museum. Your gold charm.'

'Yes. I am so sorry to bother you but I could not get in touch before. Please forgive me.' Her voice seemed to purr softly. I felt ashamed of my suspicions. 'It is very important to me. A family heirloom. I really need it now.'

'Give me your address. I'll put it in the post first thing in the morning.'

'No.' She sounded alarmed. 'I cannot risk losing it again. I must collect it from you personally.'

'Not now, it's too late.' I was beginning to feel anxious again. After all, I didn't know anything about her.

'Well, tomorrow morning will do.' She paused for a moment. 'We must meet somewhere. I shall buy you coffee.'

'OK,' I said doubtfully. I was thinking about my assignment which I'd planned to finish tomorrow. But this would be an excuse for a morning off. 'Yes. I can do that.'

'Museum Street. The coffee shop opposite the Atlantis bookshop. You know it?'

'No,' I answered, 'but I can find it. About 12?'

She hung up abruptly without saying goodbye. I suddenly realized I didn't even know her name. I felt wary. Why had I agreed to meet her? But what harm could a quick coffee do? I dug out the charm and put it by my purse. What had she called it? I couldn't remember. Anyhow, a quick coffee and I could forget all about it.

3

That night I dreamed I was back in the museum. It was dark. I was in the sculpture gallery searching for something, but I only had a small torch to see by. I thought I knew where I was going but as I flashed the light on each statue it always turned out to be the wrong one.

I was becoming more and more disorientated. I couldn't recognize any of the statues. As I went deeper into the long gallery, the more afraid I became. None of the statues here had a face. They'd all been disfigured as if something had clawed the features off, leaving only the scarred stone. I turned away and ran into a small side room. I peered into display cases where mysterious objects glimmered dimly in the darkness.

Then I realized I wasn't alone. A strange cry broke the silence. I was terrified. I ran towards the nearest door, not daring to look around me. I was sure things were moving in the shadows. I knew I had to get out of there. I threw the narrow beam of light from the torch in front of me and searched desperately for the door. There it was. I'd almost made it.

Then I saw something that sent an icy chill down my spine. My legs refused to move and I sank down to my knees. Before me the glass cases that had held twin sphinxes were completely shattered. The network of fine cracks distorted the statues within but couldn't disguise what was happening. The sphinxes had begun to move. As their heads turned towards me fragments of glass rained down onto the ground. There was nothing to hold them. They were free. I was trapped.

When I awoke it was late. I'd slept much longer than

usual. I'd have to hurry or I'd miss the meeting I'd agreed to last night. I jumped out of bed and went to open the blinds. With a start I realized there was a black cat on the narrow balcony. It stared at me and rubbed its back against the glass. I wondered how it had got there as my room is on the second floor. I started to open the window to let it out through the house, but I must have scared it. It scrambled up the wall and disappeared onto the roof.

4

I found Museum Street easily. I had been there before, without noticing its name. I'd passed the bookshop too, but this was the first time I'd actually looked in the window. It gave me a fright. All the books were on witchcraft. It was surprisingly busy. I hurried across the road where there was a row of coffee shops, looking reassuringly bright and cheerful. I was a little late myself, but she wasn't there yet.

I went in the one that seemed the most cheerful. They served large cappuccinos in brightly painted pottery cups and the other customers were youngish and smart. They were eating ciabatta sandwiches with fillings that I had only read of in magazines. I didn't have long to wait, although I hardly recognized her at first. She looked so much more sophisticated. She wore an ankle length leather coat, belted at the waist, with a long grey silk scarf wound around her neck.

She was still pale, but her face was carefully made up. Dark liner drew attention to her green eyes which seemed bright and alert. She moved as sensuously as a cat, as if she glided through life. Everyone in the café turned to look at her. She had an air of being someone special and I was pleased to be seen with her. Was this really the same woman I had helped in the museum?

She nodded at me and sat down, unbuttoning her coat. 'You've brought it?' she demanded.

'Yes, of course,' I said. 'It's in my purse.'

She held out her hand and I had no choice but to get out my purse and hand the charm over to her immediately.

'Good.' She examined it carefully, as if she feared I might cheat her, then put it in her skirt pocket. She ordered her coffee strong and black. 'In my country we don't use so much milk,' she said, smiling for the first time.

I was going to ask her where she came from, but remembered she hadn't told me her name. So I asked her this instead.

'Thanis,' she replied.

'Tanise?'

She spelt it out for me. 'It is an old family name, my grandmother was called this and her grandmother before her.'

'But you have no accent,' I said. 'Your English is really good.' This was not completely true. Her English was good, but there was something not quite right about it. She pronounced everything too carefully.

She shrugged the compliment off and asked me how my course was going. I began to tell her about college and she asked to see my sketch book, which I usually carry with me. I passed it across the table to her and tried not to watch as she turned the pages slowly. 'Yes,' she said. 'It is as I thought. You have the gift.'

I felt ridiculously pleased, as if no one had ever paid me a compliment before. I waited for her to go on but she closed the book and handed it back to me. We parted a few minutes later. I didn't look at the drawings again until I got home. I

7

could swear they had changed. They looked more finished, improved. They had more, how can I put it . . . they had more life in them.

5

I didn't expect to see Thanis again after that. I was too busy enjoying my new life in the big city to even think about her. There was so much to do, so many places to go. It was all so different from the small town where I'd grown up. Most important of all, there was Jim. We were spending more and more time together. We were full of plans for the future. Jim was going to make films, I'd be a famous artist. Everything seemed so exciting.

I'd almost forgotten all about her when a few weeks later she rang again.

'I am here for a few days. We must meet, Jessica. I have something to tell you.'

I didn't want to meet her. I tried to tell her I was too busy but she wouldn't listen.

'Of course you can make time. You must come. I have some good news for you. It will be to your advantage, I promise.'

So before I knew what had happened I'd agreed to meet her that afternoon. Despite my unwillingness, I was curious to find out what her news was. She wouldn't give me any clue on the phone. I rang Jim and told him I'd be a bit late. He wasn't very pleased, but there was nothing I could do about that.

'We were going to the cinema, remember?' he said.

'We can go to the next performance.' Actually, I'd forgotten all about the plans we'd made. There was an awkward silence.

'She's only here for a couple of days,' I excused myself. 'I couldn't get out of it. I don't want to meet her.'

'OK,' he said, but I knew it wasn't really. This was the nearest we'd ever come to an argument and as I put the phone down I felt curiously depressed.

I'd arranged to meet Thanis by the Embankment Station. I arrived a bit late, thinking to let her wait this time, but there was no sign of her when I got there. I should have been relieved, but I wasn't. I was disappointed. I promised myself that if she wasn't here in ten minutes, I'd go. It was a horrible place to wait. I had to avoid the crowds surging up from the underground and the beggars who hung around by the exits.

I was just about to give up when she arrived twenty minutes later. She looked terrible. She had bags under her eyes and seemed to have aged about ten years. This was more like the woman I had met that very first day than the sophisticated stranger who'd turned up to collect her charm.

'You must help me,' she said, without wasting any time on greetings or apologies. She took hold of my arm and began to push me towards the river. Once again, I was taken aback by her strength.

'What is it? Are you all right?' I asked, feeling a sudden wave of panic. There was a wild look in her eyes that made her seem dangerously out of place in the midst of the crowd of tourists and office workers. I could see people drawing away from us as if they feared this was yet another madwoman to be avoided. Why had I agreed to meet her? Perhaps she really was a madwoman. After all, I knew nothing about her. I wished I was with Jim. What was I doing here?

'We must go somewhere we can talk. I have something I must tell you. Here is too crowded,' Thanis whispered to me as we crossed the main road and began to walk alongside the river. Before us was the South Bank, stark and modern, with its concrete walkways and palaces of culture. To my left I could see the city where the dome of St Paul's was enclosed by towering skyscrapers. This is all real, I told myself. I'm not dreaming. I wished Thanis would let go of my arm. I felt like a prisoner.

We crossed Waterloo Bridge in silence and went down the winding stairs to the riverside walk by the film theatre. I was relieved there were lots of people around.

'Good,' Thanis said, finally dropping my arm. 'The tide is out. We can walk on the beach.'

The beach was a few feet of damp, grubby sand. I followed her down without enthusiasm, but, once there, it was as if I'd left the city far behind. Gulls screeched and swooped overhead, gentle waves lapped the shore and the river stretched what seemed a great distance to the opposite bank.

'Well,' I said doubtfully, 'what did you want to tell me?'

'You must trust me, Jessica,' Thanis said as if she could read my mind.

I said nothing, wishing I'd gone home when I still had the chance. I waited for her to continue.

'You must excuse me. I don't do things your English way. Do not forget I am a stranger here. I have to trust you too. That is not easy for me.' She seemed more relaxed now we were alone.

'I'm not like other people. My family, all of us, are different. Our culture, our religion, it is very old.' She didn't look at me as she spoke, she was gazing out across the river, a sad expression on her face.

'So where do you come from?' I asked.

'We come from the Mediterranean originally. An area you would not know,' Thanis replied. I was expecting her to tell me more, but she had fallen silent again. I found myself wondering why she always had to make such a drama out of everything.

We had walked as far as we could and turned back by an old jetty that jutted out over the beach.

'You said you had good news,' I reminded her. I was becoming impatient.

'Yes. Look, this is difficult to explain. You must be patient. It is my family. They are not modern in their ideas. They have some beliefs which seem, well, a little strange.' Thanis was choosing her words very carefully. She paused to see what effect she was having on me. I thought she was embarrassed. Well, I could sympathize with that. I think my family's strange too, so I just nodded and waited for her to go on.

'Jessica, you are an artist.'

'A student who hopes to be an artist,' I corrected her.

'Not at all. I know you have the gift. A new, young artist is just what we need. I know you can do it. I feel it here.' She raised both fists to her heart.

'Do what?' I asked, excitedly.

'You see. I told you you would be interested.' She looked around quickly and lowered her voice. 'There is a symbol which is very important to us. Here, I can show you.' She produced something from her bag. It was a page from an old book, the paper yellowed and curled at the edges. 'This is the symbol I mean.' She pointed to a small spiral, anchored by an arrow that ran through its centre.

She passed the paper to me and as I held it in my palm I felt a strange shiver of excitement, almost as if the symbol was a living thing. 'Go on,' I said, more enthusiastic now.

Thanis smiled. 'I knew you were the one,' she said. 'I knew it from the beginning, but I had to make sure. Jessica, I have a commission for you.'

'A commission? What is it?' I'd forgotten all my doubts about her now. This could be the break I'd been dreaming of. 'Come on, tell me,' I urged her.

'We are about to enter a new age. Each age has its own symbols and this spiral, we believe, will be our symbol for

11

the next millennium. We want you to make it for us. You can do it in silver.'

'But I'm not a silversmith,' I protested. 'I made some jewellery at school but I'm no expert.'

'You must believe in yourself.' Thanis smiled. 'I know you can do it.'

I looked at the picture again. It was deceptively simple. It would be difficult to achieve that purity of line. Could I really do it? 'It would take a long time,' I told her.

'I think that is not a problem. You have your summer holiday coming soon. I have the loan of a house and studio in Cornwall. We can go there together. You will love it there. It is so peaceful, so wild.' She spoke as if I had already agreed.

For a moment I was carried away by her enthusiasm, then I remembered. 'No, I can't. I've already made plans. I'm going on holiday with my friend Jim. It's all arranged. I can't let him down. Perhaps I could do it at college?'

'No, that is not possible.' She did not seem offended by my refusal. I was disappointed. I really wanted this commission.

'You will think about it. Promise me that,' Thanis insisted. And so, merely to keep her happy, I did promise.

6

I didn't expect Thanis to give up easily, but I was wrong. I didn't hear from her again that week, or the next. To be honest, I was waiting for her to phone. No one had ever commissioned a work by me before and I was flattered. It made me feel like a real artist and I had visions of a successful future where I featured on the covers of magazines and made guest appearances on TV. After all, everyone said you need both luck and talent to succeed. Why shouldn't it be me? I prayed she would ring. I was sure we could come to some other arrangement that wouldn't mean giving up my holiday with Jim.

So I was feeling more than usually optimistic. The summer term was drawing to a close, I'd got my projects finished by the deadline and had sailed through all my assessments. Jim and I had just got to the stage where we knew each other well enough to feel at ease, but not yet so well that the romance had begun to wear thin. We'd got our tickets to Athens, Factor 20 sun block, and a Rough Guide to the Greek Islands all ready to be packed.

Then, out of the blue, it happened. It was a Monday morning about ten days before we were due to leave. Jim was driving back from Liverpool after spending the weekend with his parents. The police said there must have been some oil spilled on the road, for there was no other explanation for the accident. No other vehicle was near, there were no strong winds. All Jim can remember is that his motorbike suddenly veered out of control. A witness said the bike seemed to change direction and head straight for the crash barriers that lined the middle of the road. Jim went sailing into the air, turned awkwardly, and landed on his right leg. He suffered concussion and broke his leg in two places.

At the time I wasn't suspicious. I had no reason to be. I was too worried about Jim to think of anything else. I was still upset when Thanis rang a few days later to ask if I'd changed my mind, but I agreed to go with her. To be honest, I was relieved the commission was still open. I couldn't help Jim. His parents had insisted he stay with them until his leg healed so I wouldn't see much of him until college started again in September. Now I had the chance to begin my career as an artist and spend the summer in Cornwall. After all, Cornwall was famous as a centre for the arts. I couldn't wait to go.

'I'll meet you there,' Thanis said. 'Take the 10.30 train to Penzance. Your ticket is in the post.'

'Already?'

'I had a premonition you would change your mind. I know you are perfect for this task,' Thanis replied solemnly.

I laughed and hung up. I thought I was perfect too.

7

A week later, I arrived at Penzance Station in the middle of the afternoon. Thanis wasn't there, but that didn't surprise me. She was always late. I'd give her half an hour, then I'd panic. It was near the end of July and the holiday season was in full swing. The train had been crowded with families who were now all struggling out of the station trying to juggle suitcases, prams, and the occasional surfboard. I went to get myself a drink and waited quite happily.

By the time Thanis arrived the station was empty. She looked incredibly chic, in a large sun hat and a black linen trouser suit, very plain, very expensive. Even in London she would make heads turn, down here, where most people lived in shorts and T-shirts, she looked like a star and everyone must have wondered who she was.

'Hurry up,' Thanis said. 'Let's get out of here.' She started to walk away without looking to see if I was following. I picked up my bag and hurried after her.

She'd hired a car for the summer. It was a four-wheel drive which enabled us to look down on all the lesser traffic

that filled the roads. Thanis did a U-turn out of the carpark
and turned into the main road that ran past the harbour. As
we drove along the seafront, I was filled with a sense of
adventure. I felt ready for anything. I opened the window
and let the sea breeze blow through my hair.

'You must be dying to see the studio,' Thanis said. She
didn't pause for a reply before continuing with a shudder,
'All these people. Luckily the house is very private. You will
be able to work undisturbed.'

'It's very English,' I laughed. 'The traditional seaside
holiday, buckets and spades, fish and chips, cream teas . . . '

'Ugh! Don't tell me any more. I am so glad you are here. I
cannot bear these crowds, these awful people everywhere.'

We were driving into Newlyn where the buildings were
much older. Fishing boats were anchored by the quay and
ancient warehouses lined the road. It was still a working
port with a strong smell of fish drifting in through the
window. I thought it was fascinating. Thanis was scraping
her nails on the steering wheel with a quick, clawing
movement. I could tell she was impatient to get free of the
town and its traffic.

'When you see the house you will be able to forget all this.
Our beautiful house. I know you will love it.' The traffic was
moving again. Thanis revved up the engine and the car
seemed to leap forward. Just in time, she braked inches
away from the car in front. Behind us somebody hooted
angrily. She muttered something under her breath. When, a
minute or so later, the two cars behind us collided, I was
relieved it hadn't been us.

We soon left the town behind and were driving along the
edge of the bay. Trying to appear more sophisticated, I kept
my excitement hidden. Everything was so beautiful. The sea
was a picture postcard blue and perfectly calm. The coastline
stretched away behind us and I could just see the Lizard
point in the distance. In the middle of the bay was St
Michael's Mount, a fairy tale castle which rose out of the

sea. I learned all these names afterwards. Thanis never showed the least interest in any of the tourist sites. In fact, I never discovered what she did all day long while I was working in the studio.

We soon left the busy coastal road and turned right into a network of narrow country lanes. Neither of us spoke much. It was like driving back in time. High hedges towered above us on both sides of the road. I peered through open gates into fields where golden cattle grazed peacefully or a few ponies trotted around. Tall stones were to be seen here and there. Thanis saw me looking at them and said, 'You find them everywhere. They are ancient, but they've been moved about. Now they are only good for the cows.'

'The cows?' I asked.

'They rub against them,' she said dismissively. 'They're not important any more. One day I will show you the real thing.'

I wondered what she meant by not important, but I kept quiet. I could tell she didn't share my enthusiasm for the scenery and I didn't want to start an argument. There seemed so many things she didn't like about Cornwall, I wondered what drew her here.

'We are nearly there,' Thanis said, letting out a sigh of relief.

The road wound around so much I had no idea how far we'd travelled from Penzance. We had arrived at a crossroads where we turned into an even narrower lane. She didn't slow down and I had to cling to the dashboard to stop myself from being thrown around as the car sped over the rough surface. I hoped we wouldn't meet anyone else as there was barely room for two cars to pass.

'Where exactly are we going?' I asked.

'A small cove. Not totally spoilt by tourists. There are no caravans, no camp site.'

'It's your house?' She had an annoying habit of answering questions without giving any information away.

'No. It belongs to a very old friend of mine, Eva,' she replied, putting an odd stress on very. 'You will like her. She is a painter. Very successful.'

'Oh, she's there then?' I was surprised. I thought I remembered Thanis saying the owners were away.

'No, we will be quite alone. I hope you will not be lonely?'

'I'll be too busy with my work,' I told her happily.

Thanis smiled. 'Then that is good,' she said.

We were driving through a gloomy valley, enclosed by trees on either side. Not much sunlight filtered through the dense foliage. I caught glimpses of the occasional house set back from the road. It was very quiet. After a few minutes, we parked by the roadside and went down a flight of stone steps to an old wooden door. It was set within a high wall, half hidden by a curtain of ivy.

'Here,' Thanis said, passing me a set of heavy old fashioned keys. 'Open it. I want you to feel at home.'

I don't know what I had expected, but my first sight of the house was a disappointment. As we went through the creaking door it was obvious no one had lived here for a long time. The garden was uncared for, debris littered the path and the grass in the lawn had been allowed to grow wild. I wasn't too optimistic about the house which, on first sight, seemed equally decrepit. However, I was in for a surprise when I opened the front door.

Nothing had prepared me for this. It was a complete contrast to the outside. We had entered a large living room that stretched the length of the ground floor. The walls were painted in bright, warm colours, soft oranges and reds, and hung with large, equally bright canvasses where blocks of strong colour complemented each other. Expensive designer rugs were scattered, as if casually, across the polished floorboards. It had obviously been put together by someone with flair and heaps of style. None of the colours clashed. A huge picture window had replaced the rear wall and I could just glimpse the sea through the trees. I rushed to open it

17

and, as the fresh sea air poured in I turned to find Thanis watching me closely.

'I love it!' I said.

'Of course,' Thanis replied. 'I told you you would. The house was made for an artist. It is calling for you.'

I don't know why, but I felt a shiver run up my spine. For a moment the house felt like a hungry animal, waiting to strike and gobble me up. I shuddered.

'What is the matter, Jessica?' Thanis asked.

'Oh, it's nothing.' Of course it was nothing. How could there possibly be anything wrong with this bright, modern house?

8

I wanted to phone Jim that first night, but there wasn't a phone in the house and Thanis said she had lost her mobile.

'There's a payphone by the harbour. You can walk down there later, after we've eaten. Go and unpack now. I shall make supper.'

My room looked down onto a stream that bordered one side of the long, narrow garden. It was very quiet, except for the sound of water flowing over loose stones. The furnishings were simple; bare white walls with gingham curtains and an old fashioned satin eiderdown on the high brass bed. I opened the window to let in some fresh air. The whole house had an unlived in smell. There was no sign that anyone had been here recently. I felt curious about the people who owned it. I hoped the studio would tell me more about them. I couldn't wait to see it.

Although it was still warm outside, it was very cold in here. I unpacked quickly and pulled a sweater over my head. I put my sketchbooks and pens on the bedside table, along with my camera and Walkman, then went downstairs to the kitchen where Thanis was just setting the table.

'Where's the studio?' I asked her.

'Upstairs, in the attic. Go and have a look. I think you will find everything you need,' Thanis replied. Seeing the puzzled look on my face, she continued, 'The stairs are hidden behind the door at the top of the stairs.'

A narrow flight of uncarpeted stairs led up to the attic. Cobwebs hung from the ceiling and I was sure I heard something scuttle away overhead, yet light streamed through the open doorway at the top of the stairs, enticing me to enter. The entire roof space had been converted to form a studio. Three small windows, cleverly positioned, allowed the maximum sunlight and gave a clear view of the sea. Canvasses were stacked against the far wall, loosely covered by plastic sheeting. I went towards them eagerly, dying to discover what they contained.

Dust flew up into the air as I pulled the plastic away. The first showed a storm at sea. It was filled with dark masses of cloud and shadow that made the sea seem both sinister and powerful. It wasn't what I had expected at all. It was the very opposite of the bright modern abstracts she'd hung on her living room walls. I searched in the corner for a signature and could just make out the name, Eva, followed by another I couldn't decipher.

I shrugged and turned to the next painting. Soon I was uncovering canvas after canvas. They were all of storms. There were more storms at sea, storms at midnight, dawn, and dusk. There were moorland and farmland storms. They were so bleak and gloomy I found myself shivering. But I could understand their appeal. They were very powerful. You could almost feel the wind and the rain on your face when you looked at them for long. They had a strange, timeless quality as if the artist was completely out of touch with the modern world.

I replaced the plastic sheeting and went back downstairs to the kitchen.

'So, what do you think?' Thanis asked.

For a moment I felt lost for words, then I realized she was asking me about the studio, not the paintings. 'Oh, I love it. It's so big and light.' I smiled at her, but I couldn't shake off the gloomy shadow they'd cast over me. We ate in silence. I was really hungry, but Thanis didn't seem to eat very much. She spent more time moving her food around her plate than actually eating.

After supper I walked down to the harbour. I was glad to get out of the house for a while. It was still light, but there was nobody else about. The road sloped steeply down to a small rocky beach where the Atlantic ocean crashed against the harbour walls. The scene was romantic, but also forbidding. You wouldn't stand a chance in that angry sea if your boat sank or you were swept away by a surprise wave. The harbour walls seemed a flimsy defence against the whole ocean. I couldn't bring myself to go too near the edge. It reminded me how alone I was.

There was a phone box near the harbour wall. I dialled the number quickly, longing to hear Jim's voice. His phone was engaged so I sat on a rock and gazed out to sea, watching the waves as the light faded. I tried to forget about those paintings. I started to think about my own work and was soon dreaming of fame and a new life as an artist. I'd have my own studio and my own house. I was even planning my colour scheme for the walls when a sudden movement by the water's edge brought me back to reality with a shock.

I jumped to my feet and climbed up onto the harbour wall before daring to look again. It was difficult to see clearly in the failing light, but a familiar cry stilled my panic. It was only a cat. It must have been caught off guard by a wave for its fur was wet and clinging to its sides. It stared straight at me, unconcerned and disinterested, then turned and walked back towards the cliffs at the far side of the cove. It was then I realized that we weren't alone. The whole shore was alive with movement. There were cats everywhere. They moved as silently as ghosts over the rocks and pebbles. I could sense their eyes staring at me. They were watching me, waiting. I felt mesmerized by their eyes. I couldn't move or turn away.

Without warning, a hand touched my shoulder. I nearly died with fright.

'You're wise to come out by moonlight.' It was Thanis. I hadn't heard her approach. 'It is so beautiful, so wild.'

I looked at the rocky beach. It was absolutely still. Had I imagined everything? I said nothing. I felt such a long way from everything I knew. I thought of London and my room in Camden Town. I missed my friends. I missed the crowded streets and the traffic. What if it was all a crazy dream? Did I really have the talent to make the spiral Thanis had commissioned?

'You don't have to start work tomorrow,' Thanis said softly. 'Perhaps you want to spend some time exploring. If you get up early you might avoid the crowds.'

Suddenly my doubts evaporated. 'No, I'm ready,' I said. 'I can't wait to get into the studio.' My very own studio. I could hear success calling and, more than anything, I wanted to succeed.

9

Any doubts I had soon passed. I fell easily into a routine. I'd work all day, show her my sketches and later, as the days passed, my models. She wasn't easy to please. She knew exactly what she wanted. I had to follow the original illustration she'd given me precisely. The spiral was a difficult shape to achieve and I wasn't used to working with real silver. But Thanis never seemed impatient. I was the one who was in a hurry to succeed.

I don't know what Thanis did all day long. If I asked her she'd say only 'I hid from the tourists' or 'I went for a drive'. She never volunteered any information about herself, apart from that day when we'd walked by the Thames. Looking back now, I'm amazed how little I knew about her. We spent so much time together.

She was often gone all day. I'd take my lunch out into the garden and have a solitary picnic sitting on the stone bench by the stream. Occasionally I'd catch sight of a cat slinking through the undergrowth on the opposite bank. At other times I could sense something watching me. It didn't worry me too much. I'd just cut short my break and go back to the studio. I felt safe there. It felt like my space now.

I'd moved all Eva's things to the far end of the studio, apart from one painting of the sea which I'd come to love. I was still curious about the woman who had painted it. There were few personal possessions in the house to give me a clue to her personality. I asked Thanis about her, but her answers were so vague they didn't help much. I wondered if her English was really as good as it seemed. I suspected she found conversation difficult.

One evening, when we were waiting for the sun to set so we could walk down to the harbour undisturbed by tourists, I tried again.

'So how did you meet your friends?'

'My friends?' Thanis looked puzzled.

'Peter and Eva, the people whose house this is, where did you meet them?' I asked, speaking as slowly and clearly as I could.

'A long time ago.'

'But where?' I persisted.

'Where?' She repeated the word, as if she couldn't quite understand it. After a long pause she said, 'Peter is an old friend of the family. He married Eva and became her agent. They are very busy people. They travel all over the world. I think they are in America. Eva is very talented. Just like you. You will be a success too.'

'I hope so,' I said. 'Where do they live?'

'So many questions, Jessica. Too many. You will tire me out. You will learn everything in time. For now, relax. Look how beautiful the night is. Appreciate.'

I did as I was told. I knew there was no point in asking any more questions then. She was right, the night was very beautiful. I looked out into the garden and saw the trees moving mysteriously in the breeze. Clouds raced across the sky. The stars, where they were visible, seemed so much closer than they ever do in the city.

'Come,' Thanis said. 'It is time. The moon is rising.'

10

If Thanis had ever answered all my questions, I might have forgotten about Eva and Peter. As it was, she had only succeeded in making me even more curious about them. After all, I was living in their house, using their studio. It was only natural to be interested in them. I wanted to know what they looked like. Were they young or old? Would they turn out to be as bright and fashionable as their living room? Or would they be remote and mysterious like the landscapes piled up in the studio? Eva, especially, fascinated me. She seemed to be everything I aspired to. Talented, successful, wealthy.

The next afternoon, when it was raining too heavily to go out into the garden, I decided to search for a photo of them. There had to be one somewhere. Thanis had shown me the whole house that first day and I remembered seeing a large desk in one of the two main bedrooms. There must be something in there. She'd told me to make myself at home, so I wasn't really doing anything I shouldn't. Nevertheless, I didn't want her to find me. From the upstairs window I could see that Thanis's car was not parked in its usual space and I just hoped she wouldn't come back unexpectedly.

I felt very jumpy. I could hear the rain lashing down on the roof and against the windows. Black clouds were racing across the sky. Inside the house it was very gloomy. Even switching on the lights did not seem to brighten the atmosphere much. The strange smell was much worse than usual too. The damp had intensified the mustiness and it was impossible to open the windows because of the rain.

To make matters worse, I kept thinking I could hear footsteps or doors opening. I twice rushed to the window

24

overlooking the road, expecting to see Thanis's car back in the parking place. It wasn't there. I saw only a carload of hardy holiday makers driving down to the cove. Wherever Thanis was, I was sure she would wait until the weather began to clear. But that didn't stop me feeling nervous.

I took a deep breath and pushed open the door of the main bedroom. It swung back silently, revealing a room packed with old furniture which cast deep shadows into the already crowded space. It was very airless. There was the desk I had remembered in front of the window, where, if the rain ever stopped, there must be a fantastic view. Like the rest of the furniture, it was much older than anything in the rest of the house. It made me wonder if Peter and Eva had inherited the house and, not wanting to dispose of everything, had stashed all the original furniture in here. Yet it was so out of character with the picture I'd formed of them in my imagination. It made me even more determined to search the room.

The desk was about five feet long, with a flat top, and a row of drawers at each side. It was very plain, except for the brass handles that pulled open the drawers. These were in the shape of two Chinese lions breathing flames which formed the actual handles. I went for the middle drawer first. Everything in it was very old. There were tied bundles of yellowing papers, quill pens, and ancient bottles of ink. There was no point in looking further here. I tried the top drawer on the right next. Nothing looked remotely recent here either, just some old photo albums. I opened one at random. As I'd expected, it contained only old family photographs, of no interest to anyone else. I pulled open each drawer in turn but found nothing that could possibly belong to Peter or Eva.

I was disappointed. I'd been so sure I would find something in that desk. I didn't know where to look next. Then I noticed the photograph on the mantelpiece above the small fireplace. It too had that brownish tint of very old photos, but at this distance one of the people in it really looked like Thanis. I went over and picked it up. There were three people in it. They were sitting on the stone bench in the garden. It must have been autumn because there were a lot of dead leaves around their feet. The women were wearing laced boots, a bit like the ones that were fashionable a few years ago, and high necked long dresses with heavy skirts. The man was holding a silver topped cane and had a flower in his button hole. And one of the women was the spitting image of Thanis. She had the same thick curly hair, the same sharp eyes and the same look of someone who always expects to get her own way.

I remembered I had seen some old photo albums in the desk and went back to get them out. The oldest were very ornate, embossed with gold flowers and butterflies. Sheets of tissue paper lay between each page and tiny photographs were set into oval or rectangular surrounds, also decorated with leaves and flowers. I opened one of them carefully. Many of the pictures were of strangers, mainly formal portraits of people dressed in their best and looking very uncomfortable. They must have been from the beginning of this century. There were one or two of the couple on the mantelpiece, but no more of the woman who looked so like Thanis.

I put the album down and went on to the next. It was very much the same as the first. I was about to give up and try searching elsewhere when I found her. She was on her own this time. It was taken indoors, posed on a high-backed, old-fashioned chair. There was no background, just Thanis and the chair. Why did I call her that? It couldn't be Thanis, but it was her spitting image. It couldn't even be her mother. Maybe her grandmother or great-grandmother. I remembered her explaining that she shared her grandmother's name. Perhaps they shared this incredible resemblance too.

There were six albums altogether. I looked through them all. One was set in the 1920s. Another came from the early forties, while the most recent was from the 1950s. It was fascinating to see the fashions of each period. The family was obviously well off and the women were always smartly dressed. I spread the albums on the desk top, looking through them at random.

That was how I noticed. By jumping from one album to another, from one decade to the next, it dawned on me. It wasn't just Thanis. Many of the people looked the same. It couldn't be true. It wasn't possible. But there was the man with the silver topped cane in his army uniform in India sometime during the Second World War. And there he was again, leaning against an open topped 1920s car, with a jaunty moustache and spats on his shoes. And here. In the 1950s. The fashions changed, the cars changed, the hairstyle changed, but, otherwise, the man looked exactly the same. He didn't seem to age at all. Whatever the decade, wherever the scene, he was never any older or any younger. And the same was true for the woman on the mantelpiece too.

It had to be a coincidence, but I couldn't shake off a spooky feeling. I'd forgotten all about Peter and Eva. I closed all the albums and put them back in the desk. I had to get out into the fresh air. I didn't care about the rain. I had to convince myself that the real world was still out there. That I was awake, and this wasn't all just a bad dream.

11

I spent the rest of the afternoon walking on the cliff path. The rain had eased a bit, although it was still windy. The tide was high and the sea looked spectacular, with huge waves crashing against the base of the cliffs. I was still uneasy, but the fresh air seemed to clear my mind. Everything was so healthy out here. I wasn't alone either. I passed quite a few other walkers, all wrapped up in their waterproofs, some with tents strapped to their backpacks.

I began to laugh at myself. I had let my imagination run away with me. After all, the photos were old. They weren't so clear as modern photos. Put that together with the gloomy day, the storm outside and the fact that I shouldn't have been in that room and it was easy to see how I'd jumped to all the wrong conclusions. My mother always told me I had too much imagination for my own good.

Noticing a couple coming towards me on the cliff path, I realized I'd been here two weeks and I still hadn't phoned Jim. A friendly voice was just what I needed. I turned around and headed back to the harbour. I was surprised at how many cars were lined up in the tiny carpark. I'd got so used to coming out at night that I'd forgotten all about the tourists. Unlike Thanis, I was glad they were around. They made the world seem safer and more predictable. Two children were playing at the water's edge while their parents sat reading in the front seat of their car. An elderly couple stood leaning against the harbour wall, holding a huge stripy golf umbrella over their heads.

The phone box was empty. I breathed a sigh of relief and hurried in.

'Hello, Jim?' I said as soon as someone answered at the other end.

'Who's speaking?' a stranger answered.

'Can I speak to Jim?'

'Who is this?' the voice said. 'What do you want?'

'Is that Liverpool?' I asked. I read out the number I'd dialled.

'No. It isn't,' the voice replied suspiciously before hanging up.

I was so disappointed I felt like crying. I searched for more change then tried again.

'Hello,' a cross voice now. I hung up without speaking. I checked the number although I was sure I'd dialled it right.

It must be a mistake at the exchange, I thought. I'll have to try again later.

I started to return to the house but felt strangely unwilling to go back there. Instead, I continued up the lane until I came to a junction with a tiny road I'd never noticed before. It wound down to the valley floor, crossed the stream, and meandered up the hill at the other side. There was an old mill by the stream with a hand-written sign outside advertising local pottery and free-range eggs.

I went in and pushed open the door. At first I couldn't see anyone and I was about to leave when a friendly voice shouted, 'Come in.'

A woman appeared through a door at the end of the small room where the pottery was displayed. She had spiky hair, dyed a shocking shade of red, and was dressed in army surplus trousers and an old T-shirt. I liked her immediately.

'Hi,' I said. 'Are these yours?'

'Most of them.' She smiled at me warmly and pointed to a row of mugs and jugs. 'These are how I make my living, but I do other stuff as well. It's the big pots I enjoy. Are you just passing through?'

'No, I'm here for the summer.'

'In the hotel?'

'No, I didn't know there was one. I'm staying in a friend's house. Well, a friend of a friend.' I picked up one of the jugs and admired it. The colours were so subtle. 'I'm Jessica. I make things too,' I told her.

She held out her hand. 'Melanie, Mel for short. Native of the USA as you can tell from my accent. Do you want a cup of coffee? Then you can tell me about your work. Come on through to the studio.'

Her studio was quite unlike Eva's. It was small and cluttered, with a layer of clay dust liberally scattered over everything. A small radio was playing in one corner, while

29

a kettle and two handleless mugs were next to the sink. She went over to make the coffee.

'I sell all the good ones,' she said as she passed me one of the mugs. 'Do you take sugar?'

I shook my head. I was surprised when she put three spoonfuls in her own and began to stir vigorously. She was so thin and wiry.

'A sweet tooth,' she said. 'It keeps me going.'

'Do you live here alone?' I asked.

'Not usually. My husband's away at the moment, working in Bristol. He's an architect of sorts. It gets a bit lonely. I can't shut up shop in the middle of the season.'

'Do you know a woman called Eva?' I asked her. 'A painter.'

'Why do you ask?'

'I'm staying in her house, but I've never met her. I just wondered . . .'

'Oh, I've heard of her, of course. I've never met her. She's quite reclusive. A bit weird.'

'Weird? How?' I said.

She seemed uncomfortable. 'Nothing really, you know, just gossip.'

'Her paintings are very strange,' I conceded.

'You've seen them?'

'Yes, I'm using her studio. I'm working for a friend of hers, making jewellery.'

She didn't ask me anything about my work and the conversation seemed to grind to a halt. At that moment we heard a car pull in to the driveway and she got up quickly and said, 'Customers, I hope.' I thought she seemed relieved. 'Drop in another time if you like, I'm always here.'

I followed her back into the shop area where the elderly couple I'd seen earlier were just coming in through the door. They nodded to me as I went out and I heard Mel say, 'Hi. How are you?' I paused to admire the garden where tubs of flowers were in full bloom and hens wandered freely. I

30

walked down to the stream, wishing I'd brought my camera. As I was leaving I thought I heard someone say, ' . . . in that house? Are you sure?'

'She said . . . '

'Ssh, she's still there . . . '

I turned away quickly, hoping they didn't think I was deliberately eavesdropping. I liked Mel. I wanted to come here again.

12

By the time I returned to the house I felt much better. Thanis had been shopping and, as I entered the living room, she stood up to show me the new dress she had bought. It was a silver grey crêpe, knee length, that clung slightly to her figure. She looked stunning. Stunning, but absolutely normal. How could I ever have imagined anything strange about her?

'It's time you had an evening off,' Thanis surprised me by saying. 'Let's go out to dinner.'

'Where can we go?' I asked.

'I know somewhere special. You get changed and tidy yourself up.'

'Are we going to Penzance?' I said.

'No. Somewhere you haven't been yet. No more questions. I want it to be a surprise. After all, this is your holiday too.'

Luckily, I had one dress which could pass for smart. It was black cotton and lycra, with thin shoulder straps. I painted my toenails with gold nail varnish and made up my face. I was just about to fasten my gold cross and chain around my neck when Thanis knocked on the bedroom door.

'Come in,' I shouted. She put her head around the door but would not come in. 'Are you all right? You look quite pale.'

'I will be fine,' she replied. 'I thought you would like to wear this.' She put out her hand and showed me the necklace she held. It was the gold charm I'd found that day in the museum, suspended on a fine gold chain. 'After all, we would not be here today without it. It brought us together.'

I didn't really want to wear it, but I didn't want to hurt her feelings either. 'OK,' I said and smiled, putting my cross back down. She walked into the room and fastened the charm around my neck.

'You look charming,' Thanis told me. 'Very elegant. So, are you ready?'

'Yes,' I said, thinking how she always managed to get her own way.

We got in the car and drove to St Ives. Thanis had got her colour back again and seemed quite animated. She enjoyed driving and sped fearlessly along the winding country roads. She amused me with tales about the places we passed, pointing out houses where various artists had lived. We found a parking space easily, luckily someone was just leaving as we arrived, and parked near the harbour.

After two weeks spent hard at work in my studio, St Ives was really exciting. There was a maze of ancient narrow streets and, at every turning, fantastic views out over the bay. The rain had finally stopped and the sky was a clear blue flushed with pink. The town was busy, with groups of holidaymakers strolling through the cobbled streets and stopping to look in the windows of the many small galleries where local artists exhibited their work.

Unusually, Thanis seemed to be in no hurry to get away from the crowds.

'One day you will have your work displayed here,' Thanis told me.

'I hope so,' I replied.

'Oh, I'm sure.' Thanis smiled. 'You will succeed if you really want to, Jessica.'

'I want to be very successful. Rich and Famous.' I laughed, but I really meant it. It had always been my dream. I wasn't content to live in a small town and be like other people. I wanted to be different. I wanted to be a success more than anything else in the world. Unlike my parents, Thanis always encouraged my ambition. I felt she wanted the credit of discovering me. I didn't mind. I owed her so much.

We ate in a quiet restaurant in a large stone building that had once been a boathouse. It was very expensive. The tablecloths were a thick linen and candles glowed discreetly on each table. Tasteful abstract paintings hung on the walls. Everyone looked very cultured, with the easy manners of people accustomed to getting the best out of life. I really loved it.

'It's perfect,' I said. 'Thank you very much for bringing me here.'

'I knew you would like it. It's the sort of place you belong. Let us drink to your future.'

As we drove home that night, I hadn't a care in the world. The panic of the afternoon was completely forgotten. I was happy. I was going to get what I wanted out of life. Nothing could stop me. I was on my way.

13

It had been a perfect evening. I went to bed in a good mood, so I don't know why I had such bad dreams. It was as if all the fears I'd pushed to the back of my mind came rushing back as soon as I shut my eyes. I found myself in the museum again, but this time I wasn't a visitor. I was one of the exhibits. I was sitting on a stone plinth, unable to move or speak. Strangers walking past stopped to stare at me. I could hear them whispering but I couldn't catch their words.

After a while the gallery began to empty. I felt as if I'd been there for centuries. At last, I heard footsteps in the distance. I hoped someone was coming to set me free. I was disappointed. Two workmen arrived carrying large panes of glass which they started to screw together with shiny silver brackets. They worked in silence.

When they had finished, they lifted it up and lowered it over my head. I wanted to scream but no sound came out. I was helpless. All hope faded as the workmen went away. I could hear their footsteps fading into the distance. Then the lights went out. The room was completely dark. It was silent. But not for long. Soon there were other footsteps. Not human footsteps. A soft, padded sound. Like an animal out hunting. I knew it was coming for me. I couldn't see anything, but I could hear it breathing. It was getting closer. And I was powerless to resist.

I woke up sweating and desperate for fresh air. The room was stuffy and had that strange smell I'd noticed before. I wondered if one of the stray cats sometimes managed to get in when the house was empty. It was definitely a catlike smell. I could hear that the weather had changed again by the sound of the leaves being tossed around by the storm. I went over to the window intending to open it wide and let the full force of the wind rush into the room. I don't know what instinct made me look down. My hand dropped from the catch and I moved back behind the curtain. Someone was out there. I was sure it wasn't just the shadows playing tricks on my eyes. Someone was there.

I waited a few seconds while I got used to the dark then looked again. I could see now that it was Thanis, sitting on the stone bench by the stream. She was as still as a statue and seemed to be gazing up at the sky, watching the clouds race past the moon. Her pale skin gleamed in the moonlight. She looked as though she'd gone out on impulse, stopping only to tie a sheet around her. Her hair hung loose down her back. I realized it was much longer than it seemed when she had it tied back in her usual style. Her feet, as far as I could tell, were bare. I knew she mustn't see me.

What was it about Thanis that held me there, fascinated? Too late, I saw something else move in the shadows. Two figures emerged from the trees and joined her on the bench. No one spoke. I couldn't see their features clearly, but it looked like a man and a woman. Did I make a sound or give myself away? I don't know. All I know is that suddenly, in unison, their heads turned and they stared straight at me. I swung back against the wall and held my breath. Whatever happened, I did not want to meet their eyes. All my instincts shouted that I was in danger. I shivered. After a few minutes I circled my way round the outskirts of the room back to my bed.

I lay awake for hours. Had I really seen what I'd thought I'd seen? Had there really been a moment when the moon was free of cloud and I could see the faces more clearly? Or had I just imagined that they were the same faces I'd seen before, seen so many times in all those photographs that I'd found in the desk drawer?

14

The next day it rained incessantly. I could hear it drumming against the window and the studio roof. I couldn't concentrate on my work. Nothing would go right. My hands were so clumsy that I damaged the piece of silver which I was trying to beat into a gentle curve. You have to really concentrate. You have to get a rhythm and keep the hammer blows regular. I couldn't do it. When I hit my fingers for the umpteenth time I gave up. I was too tired from my lack of sleep the night before, too confused by all the strange things that had been happening in the last twenty-four hours. It was so dark in the studio too. It felt as if the day hadn't managed to break properly and the world was stuck in a gloomy, in-between state, neither night nor day.

I knew I had to get out of the house, whatever the weather. I decided to cycle down to the payphone and telephone Jim. I needed to speak to him. I needed him to laugh at my fears and reassure me that it was all my overactive imagination. He was my only contact with the normal world where things went on just as usual and strange things only happened on late night TV. I think I needed to convince myself that that world still existed.

I found an old nylon mac in a cupboard. It was miles too long, but it would keep me fairly dry. I changed into my cycling shorts and a T-shirt and went out to get the ancient bicycle which I'd seen in the garden shed. It was a bit too big for me and very uncomfortable, but I managed to stay on as I steered my way down the bumpy lane to the sea.

Even on a day like this, the seafront wasn't deserted. There were a few cars in the carpark, and a few determined people gazing at the waves through their windscreens. There was even somebody in the phone box, and I had to wait, rain running down the back of my neck and whipping against my face, while a man tried number after number, apparently finding nobody in.

I half expected the same thing to happen to me. It was a relief to hear Jim's mum answer the phone and pass it over to him.

'Hi, Jess, how's life in the fast lane?'

I was so happy to hear his voice. How long was it since I'd spoken to him? Too long. I'd been so preoccupied with myself that I'd almost forgotten about him and my life in London.

'Not so exciting, but I'm working hard,' I told him.

'Are you all right, you sound a bit strange?' he asked.

I paused, unsure what to say. Should I tell him everything? I wanted to, but it wasn't easy to put my fears into words. After all, nothing had really happened. A few old photographs, some shadows in the garden. I couldn't even be sure last night wasn't all just another bad dream. Maybe I'd been asleep the whole time. 'I'm fine,' I said. 'Just a bit tired. I didn't sleep very well last night. The weather's awful. It kept me awake.'

'Poor you. Miss me?' he asked.

I hesitated. I was missing him now. His voice brought him so close, yet he was still so far away. I remembered how cute he looked in his motorbike leathers, his curly hair ruffled and flattened by his helmet. But I wasn't going to tell him that. I didn't want to put him off.

'How are you?' I asked. 'Can you walk yet?'

'Not far,' he answered. 'It'll be weeks before the plaster comes off. At least I'm building up my muscles by using crutches.' He laughed. I realized I hadn't laughed since I'd been here. I couldn't even imagine Thanis laughing. 'I'm really bored.' He lowered his voice. 'One more episode of *Coronation Street* and I'll go mad. I can't wait to get back to London.'

'Me too,' I said, really meaning it.

'You're not bored with the artist's life already? I don't believe that. I just wish I could join you.'

'So do I. I'd love to see you,' I said.

'You could take a few days off. Come up here.'

I was tempted, but it was so far to travel and Thanis might think I was ungrateful. I didn't want to offend her. 'I can't,' I told him regretfully. 'I have to finish my work.'

'How's it going?' he asked.

'Not bad. I've finished my initial drawings and I'm working on the spiral now. I'm getting used to heating the silver. That's the scary bit. I've got to use this gas and air torch with an enormous flame.'

'You can do it. You have to believe in yourself, Jess.'

'That's what Thanis says, too.'

'How are you getting on with her? Are you two alone down there?'

'Yes, although I met another woman yesterday. She runs a pottery. It's . . . ' I hesitated. ' . . . a bit strange here with Thanis. I don't see much of her during the day. It gets quite lonely,' I finished lamely.

'Look, give me your address. I'll write,' Jim said. 'You sound as if you need cheering up.'

I had started to give him the address when the pips sounded. I had another 50p ready and had just pushed it into the slot when the line went dead. I was cross. That was the last of my change. We hadn't even said goodbye.

I don't know what made me look up at just that moment. Perhaps it was the sound of a bigger than usual wave breaking over the harbour wall. Or maybe some movement caught in the corner of my eye. But this time I do know that what I saw was real. One minute the harbour wall was empty, the next, a wave broke and it was submerged beneath the foaming water. Then, when it drained back again, there was Thanis walking slowly towards the land, looking cool and unruffled despite the wind, rain, and raging waves. She was wearing dark trousers beneath a short, black shiny mac and her hair was tied in a tight knot at the back of her head. And she wasn't alone. Her arm was linked with a tall, elderly man who held a huge umbrella over both their heads. His hair was streaked with grey, but his piercing eyes were still bright and full of life.

For some reason I didn't want to tell Thanis about my phone call to Jim, so I hoped they wouldn't see me. But there wasn't anywhere to hide. I saw her pointing at me and had no choice but to open the phone box door and walk out into the rain to meet them.

'So this is the next artist?' the stranger said, holding a hand out to me. He spoke with a heavy accent and I wondered if he'd really meant what he said. He gripped my hand and held on to it a moment too long. It made me feel uncomfortable. As our palms touched I felt how cold and dry his was. His skin felt like paper. I had to force myself not to shudder. 'Thanis has been telling me how talented you are.'

'I'm trying,' I said with false modesty. Water was dripping from their umbrella onto my hair. I wondered who he was, and what his connection with Thanis was.

'A typical English summer,' he smiled, gesturing to the wild scene all around us. The tide was coming in fast, with more and more high waves breaking over the harbour walls. The surface of the water was a seething mass, lacerated by the fierce rain. I wondered how they had kept so dry. Even a large umbrella didn't seem much defence against the way the elements were raging that day. Thanis was gazing out to sea with a rapt expression on her face. She was trying not to show it, but I could see she was in an unusual state of excitement. I realized she was daring the waves to get higher and wilder. I think she would have liked to see them sweep away the harbour walls altogether, and send the carpark, cars, and their occupants straight to the bottom of the ocean.

'Allow me to introduce myself,' the stranger said. 'I'm

Nuskhet Harsie, Thanis and I are very old friends.' At that, they both turned to each other and exchanged a smile, as if they were sharing a secret joke. He continued, 'Thanis has great expectations of you. I hope you will not disappoint her.' His eyes seemed to bore into me as if he could extract any secrets I might be harbouring. I felt uncomfortable and looked to Thanis for support. She said nothing. I sensed that she was tense too.

'Well,' I said at last, 'I will do my best.' I turned away quickly and walked over to my bike. I waited until I was well on my way before turning back to wave goodbye. I wondered if they were returning to the house. Would he ask to see my work? Visit my studio? No, I couldn't bear that. There was something about him that gave me the creeps. I realized how little I still knew about Thanis. Was there something in her background she was trying to hide? If it involved Nuskhet, I didn't blame her.

15

I decided to cycle up to the pottery to visit Melanie. I'd stay away from the house for as long as I could. Hopefully, Nuskhet would be gone by the time I returned. As I cycled up the drive I was relieved to see Melanie's windows blazing with light. She laughed when she saw me dripping all over her doorstep.

'Come in,' she said. 'Here, give me that. I'll hang it in the shower. You look half drowned.' She took my oversized plastic mac and came back with a towel. 'Where have you been?'

'Not far, just down to the phone,' I told her.

'Haven't you got one in the house?'

'No. It's a nuisance. I wanted to phone my friend in Liverpool. It's the first time I've managed to get through to him.'

'You're really cut off in that house, aren't you? You don't mind?' Melanie asked.

'Most of the time I'm too busy working, so it doesn't bother me. It's just days like this. It's so dark in my studio. I had to get out.'

'You can always use my phone. Any time. I'd go mad if I didn't talk to my friends every day. Living in a place like this, you have to keep in touch.'

'Thanks. I will.' I finished towelling my hair and followed her into the living room. We sat down by a large table which overlooked the old waterwheel in the back garden. A couple of ducks were sheltering under a small tree that grew by the water's edge, but there was no sign of the hens I'd seen on my first visit. 'Your garden's lovely,' I said. 'Have you lived here long?'

'Two years, but I've been in England for five. I came for a holiday and stayed. My husband's English,' she said. 'We'll move on eventually, when we've finished restoring the mill. I love it here but it's so isolated. People who stay here too long go a bit crazy. There's some real weirdos living up on the moor. Have you been up there?'

'No, I haven't really been anywhere much. I've only been here two weeks,' I told her.

'You must. It's like another world.' She paused. 'They say there's a wild cat loose up there. No one knows what it is or how it got there. Or if it really exists.'

'No one's seen it?' I asked.

'People have seen it. But no one's managed to bring back any proof. You should read the letters page in the local paper. One swears he's seen a puma, another a lion. It seems to change its shape from one week to the next.' She

41

laughed, then her expression grew suddenly serious. 'I've enough trouble with the cats.'

'I've seen them,' I said, 'on the beach. They're creepy.'

'You have? Not many people see them. They only come out at night. But you hear them. I used to keep doves. They got them all. It was awful.' She fell silent. I could see she was remembering. She shuddered. 'Well, they won't get the hens. I'll make sure of that. I must give you some eggs. They're real fresh country eggs.'

'Thanks. Is this rain ever going to stop? It seems to be getting worse. I'm not stopping you working?' I was still unwilling to go back to the house. I felt really at ease here.

'No. I needed a break. Anyhow, I can work and talk. You might have noticed, I talk rather a lot.'

'You've really cheered me up,' I said. 'I needed to get away from the house.'

She looked at me enquiringly. 'Is everything OK? You can always stay here if it isn't. I'd be glad of the company.' She held out her hand and touched my knee lightly.

I smiled. 'It's nothing really. But thanks for the offer. It's my first commission. I feel a bit anxious. And I have been alone a lot.'

'You're not staying there alone?' she asked, looking worried.

'No, Thanis is there. But she's out most days and she's not really a friend. I can't relax with her.'

'Look, Jessica, if anything happens you come straight here. Promise.'

'OK, but nothing will happen. I'm fine, really. If the sun shines tomorrow I'll be on top of the world again.'

I stayed there for hours and by the time I left we felt like old friends. The rain didn't stop. I left my bike in her outhouse and Mel gave me a lift home in her battered old Mini. As she pulled up outside I said, 'Do you want to come in? I could show you the studio.'

She shook her head. 'Another time. I'll see you soon? Good.'

I got out of the car and, holding the mac over my head, hurried down the stone steps that led to the garden door. I pushed the door open and turned to give her a last wave before going in.

At first sight, the house was in darkness. Again, I had the impression that it was unlived in and uncared for. Then I realized a faint beam of light was falling into the living room from the kitchen. Thanis must be in. I walked up the path, being careful not to slip on the wet stones. I could hear the stream rushing down to the sea. It was so much louder than usual that I had to go and have a look. I walked around the house and stood by the water's edge. It was hard to believe it was the same stream. The water level was much higher and threatened to overflow into the garden. It was so fast too.

Two oblongs of light fell from the kitchen windows. I hoped Thanis wasn't worrying about me. I had been out a long time. I turned to look into the room and could just see her. She seemed to be alone. That was a relief. I was about to go in when I realized she had started talking. Surely Nuskhet wasn't still there? As if she had sensed someone watching she walked up to the window and looked out. Without thinking, I drew back. Then I saw a shadow move behind her. It seemed to be a cat.

16

'Hello,' I shouted as I opened the front door. 'I'm back.'

'In the kitchen,' she replied.

'What a night. I can't believe this is summer,' I said. I looked around the room for the cat. I couldn't see it.

'Enjoyed yourself?' she asked.

'Yes, I've made a friend. I couldn't work in this weather. Too dark. I need good light.'

'You met Melanie.'

'You know her?' I was surprised.

'No, but we saw your bike in her drive when we passed.'

'You went out walking?' I asked in amazement.

'No, we went for a drive. We looked for you. I thought you might want to go to Penzance. You haven't been out much. Anyway, it doesn't matter. So long as you were happy,' Thanis said. 'Here, I made some soup.' She passed me a bowl of steaming broth. 'Do you like it?'

'What is it?' I asked. It had a taste I couldn't recognize.

'It's a wild herb recipe. Nuskhet brought me the herbs. They're very hard to find in this country.'

'You're not eating?'

'I've eaten already.'

I finished the soup and started to feel sleepy. After being with Mel all day, I found it quite hard to talk to Thanis. She was always friendly, but so self-contained that the conversation never developed beyond polite statements. If she wouldn't talk about herself I'd never get to know her better.

'I think I'll have an early night,' I told her. 'I can't keep my eyes open.'

'You do that. Sleep well, Jessica. And dream.'

I did sleep well. And dream. Strange, confused dreams. I think I lived a hundred different lives that night. I woke up with my head full of a thousand images, but by the time I'd washed my face I couldn't remember any of them.

17

Nuskhet invited us to lunch at his house a few days later. I didn't want to go, but Thanis overruled me.

'Don't be a fool, Jessica. Nuskhet can be very useful to you. If you are going to be successful, you will have to learn to cultivate such contacts,' she told me.

'But I'm really busy. I just want to be left alone to work,' I said unhappily. I hadn't forgotten my aversion to Nuskhet and decided to put up a fight.

Thanis gave me a meaningful look that made clear her disbelief. I remembered the time I'd spent with Mel or out walking. I realized I was never going to win a contest of wills with her.

'We won't stay long. You'll enjoy the drive. The scenery is very special where he lives. You will come. I don't want to offend him,' Thanis said and walked off before I could disagree further.

'An hour, OK,' I shouted after her.

So, later that week, I found myself sitting next to Thanis as she sped away from the house. I was still in a bad mood so didn't say anything and an uncomfortable silence prevailed. She seemed to know the route well as she turned easily into tiny side roads half hidden by tall Cornish hedges. The land got higher as we drove further inland and, looking back, I had a clear view of the ocean and the whole coastline. We soon left the fields behind and came out onto open moorland where roadsigns warned us of stray cattle. The road was so narrow our big car kept overshooting its surface and bumping across thick clumps of gorse and bracken.

I had no idea where we were, or even what direction we'd taken. I was surprised when, suddenly, I saw the sea before me and we began to descend towards it. Nuskhet's house seemed perched on the edge of a headland, with stunning sea views from three sides. As we got out of the car I could just glimpse a beach below where there were the ruins of a tiny stone cottage. I couldn't imagine who would have lived there, it was such a desolate spot.

Thanis seemed preoccupied. She kept looking around with a worried expression on her face.

'Is anything wrong?' I asked her.

'No, nothing. Why should anything be wrong?' she snapped as she slammed the car door. 'Hurry up. We mustn't be late.'

The road ended some distance from the house and we had to follow a rough, stony footpath to get to the front door. As I hurried after her I could hear the sea crashing onto the rocks below us. The wind whipped my hair across my face and I had difficulty seeing where I was going. I wondered why anyone would choose to build a house here.

'How long has he lived here?' I asked. 'Does he live here all the time?'

'Always questions. This is not the time, Jessica. If you really want to know these things, you must ask Nuskhet yourself. Now, it's better not to talk. Just concentrate on walking and we will get there faster.'

We were both in bad moods when we finally reached the house. It was built of the local granite and had a cold, unwelcoming look. It was very plain. That was why I was so surprised when, on reaching the front door, I looked up to find a stone lion's head at the edge of the roof. The door was opened immediately, but not by Nuskhet himself. An elderly woman, her hair dyed a too-harsh shade of black, showed us in without speaking. We followed her down a narrow, stone-flagged corridor into a room at the back of the house which overlooked the sea.

I must have gasped out loud, for Nuskhet, leaning forward from the winged chair where he sat, said, 'Yes, it is splendid. The whole of the Atlantic Ocean lies before you. The source of all life, as your scientists now tell us.'

'Where are we exactly?' I asked.

'At the edge of the world,' he replied with the glimmer of a smile in his eyes. 'Not far from Land's End.' He chuckled at his own joke and I forced myself to smile.

'It's so different here,' I said.

'You have crossed the peninsula. Here the land is unspoilt. It has been so for thousands of years.' He got to his feet slowly, moving as if he was in great pain. 'Come, it is time for lunch. Everything is ready.'

As he came towards me, I found myself involuntarily drawing back. I turned quickly, hoping he would not catch the expression of revulsion on my face. Thanis had moved over to the window, where she stood with her back towards us. Now she walked across to Nuskhet and took his arm. I saw him straighten immediately and his steps became easier. I followed them into a small dining room at the side of the house.

The table was set for a formal meal and my heart sank. It was laid with heavy silver cutlery and stiff linen napkins. It reminded me of still lives I had seen in old master paintings. Beautiful, but gloomy. We ate soup, followed by fish with rice and lentils. The meal seemed to last forever, despite Nuskhet's efforts to be the perfect host. He tried to entertain us, but I sensed something false about his good humour. My opinion of him hadn't changed. I was sure something was wrong. They were hiding something from me.

47

As soon as the meal was over I made some excuse and went outside to get some fresh air. I was surprised how warm it felt. Inside, the dining room had been really chilly, perhaps because the heavy velvet curtains kept out the sun. I walked across the wild garden to the tip of the headland from where I had an uninterrupted view of the Atlantic Ocean. I climbed down the cliff a short distance and sat on a large granite boulder, wishing I had brought my sketchbook with me. I watched the gulls swooping over the sea and began to relax. If only I was there in different circumstances. I imagined having Jim by my side and closed my eyes to get a better picture of his face. To my horror, I couldn't remember it at all. It was as if he'd never really existed. London, and all that life, were so far away. They seemed like a dream.

The sound of the waves was almost hypnotic. I had to force myself to open my eyes. If I went to sleep now I might never wake up again. This place would cast a spell over me and I'd be changed to a strange shaped stone like the girls in one of the local legends Mel had told me. I went back to the house, determined it was time to leave, but there was no sign of Thanis and Nuskhet. I shouted loudly. I felt unwilling to enter any of the rooms. I expected someone to answer, if only the servant, but no one did. The silence was unnerving, it was so complete. I went back out again and decided to try and find a way down to the beach.

Despite a thorough search, I couldn't find a track down the cliffs. There had to be a way, because of the ruined cottage. Maybe it had been lost in a landslide? I decided to climb down instead. It was harder than it looked. Although the blocks of granite sometimes formed a series of giant steps, in other places the recent rain had made the ground treacherously slippy. I skidded a few feet more than once, and on one occasion only an outcrop of rock stopped me sailing into space. I'd scraped the skin from my palms and was sure my knees would be covered in bruises tomorrow.

But I made it. I walked over the rocks to the water's edge with a sense of achievement. Despite everything, I was glad I was here. It was stunning. Thanis had been right that I would love it. I did.

Later, I'd look for an easier route back up the cliff. Now, I just wanted to explore and enjoy my solitude. There was plenty here to inspire an artist. I was sure I'd get some good ideas for future work. It was surprisingly sheltered down here. I felt quite hot. On an impulse, I decided to swim. There was no one to see me so I undressed quickly and began to wade into the water. It was icy cold. The waves broke around my legs, almost forcing me back to shore, but beyond them was a calmer area of water and I persevered. I felt invulnerable, as if nothing could harm me.

Suddenly, I reached a gap in the rocks and the ground fell away steeply. I started to swim and crossed the narrow bay from side to side. The cold was so intense I was totally unaware of everything around me and had just decided I couldn't bear it any longer when, to my amazement, I heard voices.

I looked around, but couldn't see anyone. Had I imagined it? No, there it was again. Distorted, but definitely a voice. I half expected to see a mermaid, combing her hair on a rock. No, nothing. Where was it coming from? I began to feel nervous. I was so isolated down here. No one knew where I was. I climbed out of the water quickly onto the rocks. I listened carefully but could hear nothing now. There must be someone here, just out of sight.

I went back to the beach and dried myself as well as I could with my T-shirt. I pulled on my jeans and sweater and squeezed the water out of my hair. I looked around. There was still no one in sight. I worked my way carefully around the rocks, going far out towards the open sea. The sea was much rougher here and spray drifted over from where the waves were breaking a few yards away. I shivered, although the sun was warm and my hair had

49

begun to dry. The rocks were slippier now, coated with a thick layer of seaweed among which mussels and scallops were hidden. I wondered if I should turn back, but I really wanted to know what I had heard. Also, when I looked up, I could see that the land dropped near the headland. It would be much easier to climb up there than back at the beach.

I was about to give up and start the long climb back to Nuskhet's house when a flash of light caught my eye. I moved towards its direction and discovered a narrow entrance into a cave. I just managed to squeeze through. Inside was a large open space where the sound of the waves was magnified eerily. There was a deep drop down to where the occasional wave rolled in, but the surfaces all around me were slimy and damp. I realized the whole cave would be flooded at high tide.

It was very dark inside. After a few moments my eyes adjusted to the gloom. I could see the space narrowed again a few yards away. I started to move towards it, thinking I would just try and see what was beyond. All of a sudden, a beam of light swung out into the darkness. It gave me such a shock that I swung back instinctively. I lost my footing and I slipped down towards the water. I was terrified. I thought I'd had it. I imagined myself lost in those dark swirling waters and I screamed as loud as I could.

I looked up to see the light searching just above me. I couldn't believe my luck. Someone was really here. Just then, I landed with a splash in the freezing water and a jolt of pain shot through my body. I struggled to regain my balance, reaching out desperately to find a surface to cling to. At last, my fingers found a clump of limpets that allowed me a grip. Luckily for me, the water was less deep than I had imagined. It barely reached my knees.

'Over here,' I shouted. 'I'm here, in the water. Help. Help. I can't get out.' I thought I'd broken my ankle, the pain was so intense. I couldn't put any weight on my left foot at all.

'Jessica, is that you?' The voice belonged to Thanis. I heard someone else speak and was amazed to see both her and Nuskhet peer over the edge, pointing a torch down onto my face. I was so relieved that someone had found me that I didn't wonder how they had got there.

'Help, help,' I continued to shout unnecessarily.

'Just a minute, I'll get you out,' Thanis said calmly. 'Work your way over here, it's easier.'

'I can't,' I said pathetically. 'I can't walk at all.'

'Of course you can. It's not far.'

'Shall we . . . ' Nuskhet began to say.

'Ssh,' Thanis commanded. 'She'll do as I say. Wait there. Now come on, Jessica. You can do it.'

Putting all my weight on my one good foot and my hands, I began to move slowly towards Thanis. She encouraged me as if I was a child taking my first steps. I felt absurdly pleased with myself. I think I was still too shocked to think straight.

At last, I reached her and was able to grip the hand she stretched down.

'What are you doing here?' she asked as she pulled me up. I must have lost all sensation in my body because I couldn't feel a thing. It all seemed so easy. One minute I was still in the dark, icy water, the next I was standing on dry rock beside her.

'Leave her,' Nuskhet said. 'Look how she is shivering. We must get her home quickly.'

'She is fine, don't fuss,' Thanis said rudely. I was amazed at her tone. She seemed to have taken control of us all.

'Allow me,' Nuskhet said, taking hold of my ankle. In the half light he didn't look nearly so old. His eyes were full of compassion and I wondered why I had disliked him so. I stopped shivering immediately. His hand felt warm on my ankle and the pain I'd felt earlier seemed to dull.

'It is not broken now,' he said. 'You can walk.'

'We must hurry,' Thanis said. 'The tide is coming in.'

51

The water had risen incredibly quickly. I didn't want to think about what might have happened if I'd still been stuck down there. I turned away and followed them to the back of the cave. I was surprised how easy it was. There was a narrow strip of footpath that was dry and clear of seaweed. It led to a couple of steps that took us out of the cave and into a tunnel that zigzagged upwards. I followed passively, finding it easier to walk than I had expected. Thanis held the torch, keeping the light straight ahead of us. Even so, every now and then I caught glimpses of other tunnels leading off to the darkness. Once I thought I saw a flickering light.

'What's that?' I asked.

'What?' Thanis replied.

'That light,' I said.

She hurried on. 'It's nothing. Only a reflection. Don't waste time.'

I looked behind, but couldn't see anything now. The darkness behind us was absolute and it was hard to believe we'd really passed through it. Only the strange booming noise below us was a reminder of the incoming sea. After a few more twists and turns we finally saw daylight. We had to climb out of the tunnel mouth, which was hidden among a large group of granite rocks that were just below Nuskhet's house.

'That was a lucky escape,' I said.

'Luck? No, luck had nothing to do with it,' Thanis said.

'I didn't mean . . . ' I stuttered. 'I meant to thank you.'

'Don't bother,' Thanis said. 'If you want to kill yourself that is your affair.'

'What were you doing there?' I said, but Thanis had already gone too far ahead to hear.

'Come along,' Nuskhet told me. 'You need a hot drink. I believe you are in a hurry to get home.'

I walked back to the house with him, slowing my pace to match his. Here in the daylight, I could see how painfully he moved. The darkness must have deceived me earlier, when he seemed much quicker. We walked in silence. It was only later, in bed that night, that I started to think over everything that had happened that afternoon. Had I been wrong about him? I wasn't sure.

18

I slept soundly that night. When I got up the next morning Thanis was waiting in the kitchen, a pot of coffee and two mugs ready on the table.

'Good morning.' She smiled. She seemed in an unusually good mood. She poured out the coffee and started to slice bread for toast. 'How are you this morning? Sleep well?'

'Yes I did. I was out like a light. It must be all that fresh air we had.'

'Perhaps. And how is your foot?' she asked.

'My foot?' I'd almost forgotten about my accident yesterday. 'It seems fine. It doesn't hurt at all.'

'You can thank Nuskhet for that,' Thanis told me.

'Nuskhet?' I was puzzled.

'He was a famous healer in his day. He still has the power, although he cannot use it much. He is no longer strong enough. Such great age is a burden.'

'How old is he?' I asked, trying to change the subject. I didn't believe in healers, but didn't want to offend her. As usual, it wasn't easy to hide anything from her. My face must have betrayed me for she said:

'Jessica, you are such a sceptic. You told me yourself you had broken something.'

'And you assured me I hadn't.'

'Have it your own way,' she said sulkily, 'but you will never be a great artist if you insist on being so narrow minded.' With that she flounced out of the kitchen, leaving me to rescue the burning toast.

I took my breakfast up to the studio. I didn't want to waste any time before starting work. But it was hard to concentrate. I couldn't get Thanis's words out of my head. It was true my foot did not hurt at all. That was strange. It wasn't even bruised or swollen. I remembered how the pain had stopped when Nuskhet had put his hand around it. It seemed crazy. I couldn't accept it had been broken, but maybe he did have some sort of healing power.

Gradually the work took my mind off everything else. There was something soothing about the rhythm of the hammer as I slowly beat the silver into the shape I wanted. I worked all morning. I'd become more confident and was enjoying what I was doing. The spiral would be finished soon. I'd be able to leave and go back to London. To my surprise, I found the thought depressing. Jim wouldn't be there. I'd be just another art student. The brilliant future I'd been dreaming of might fade away. I realized how dependent I'd become on Thanis's support and encouragement. But what if she was wrong? What if I was just ordinary?

Luckily, my thoughts were interrupted by a knock at the studio door. It was Thanis.

'I think we should take the afternoon off,' she said. 'You haven't seen much of Cornwall.'

That was true. Apart from yesterday, I had spent most of my three weeks here indoors, with only short walks down to the cove or along the cliffs. I hadn't done any sightseeing. 'But where can we go that won't be full of tourists?' I asked, knowing how much she hated the crowds.

'I know somewhere you will love. An artist needs inspiration, is that not so? And I know the perfect place.' This light-hearted mood was untypical and I was happy to go along with it. I thought she was trying to make the peace after our disagreement that morning. 'So, is it a good idea?' Thanis asked. Without waiting for a reply she continued, 'Then you must finish here and get ready.'

19

In the end, it was Thanis who was not ready. I waited out by the stream while she did whatever it was she had to do to look as immaculate as she always did. I noticed the cats had been in the garden again. The bare earth under the seat was full of claw marks. I wondered if anyone looked after them, or if they were completely wild. I knew there were plenty of feral cats in the city, maybe they were spreading through the countryside too.

It was nearly three when we finally set off. Thanis still wouldn't tell me where we were going. She insisted she wanted it to be a surprise. We didn't take the car. Instead, we walked away from the sea and turned into the side road that passed Mel's pottery. Her car wasn't in the drive and I wondered where she'd gone. It wasn't like her to shut up shop for no reason.

Thanis walked quickly and I had no time to worry about Mel. We crossed the stream and were soon climbing the steep hill at the other side. There was more of a village than I had realized. We passed picture postcard cottages, with immaculate gardens and Land Rovers parked, clean and shining, in the drives. There was only one working farm, whose yard and barns were muddy and dilapidated. Here an angry dog rushed out, barking fiercely, to chase us away.

It seemed to change its mind, for it soon gave up and retreated, tail between its legs.

'Stupid creatures,' Thanis said.

It wasn't long before we left the houses behind us and the lane narrowed. We had to avoid patches of deep mud left by the heavy rains of a few days ago. I was surprised at how quickly Thanis walked. Despite her thin sandals she seemed to glide over the rough surface as easily as if she was spending the afternoon shopping in the King's Road. I was much slower. My walking boots were thick with mud which had also splattered my jeans. Thanis still looked as fresh and immaculate as when we had started out.

Towards the top of the hill, we turned onto a footpath which ran along the edge of the fields. Thanis strode ahead. I was having trouble keeping up. She seemed to pick her way through the ruts and deep mud without having to watch where she put her feet. There were a few cattle grazing at the top of the field, but when they saw us approaching they ran away in alarm.

We crossed a stone stile in the boundary wall and found ourselves in a much rougher terrain. The grass gave way to bracken and gorse and I was glad my legs were protected by my jeans. The path had narrowed, and, at times, seemed to disappear completely. I had to pick my way through as best I could. There was a spectacular view over to the ocean. The village had sunk out of view and it was hard to believe it was only an hour's walk away.

Here and there, huge blocks of granite broke the surface. To me they were more exciting than any sculpture. There was something prehistoric about them. They had probably been there for millions of years, long before there were cities and roads and all the other things we take for granted. Different kinds of moss and lichen had grown over their surfaces. When I looked closely I was amazed by how many colours I could see there. Reds, purples, greens, oranges, and yellows.

Thanis stretched out her arms. There was a look of complete contentment on her face, like a cat about to purr. 'So, what do you think? I was right?' she said softly.

'I had no idea there was anything like this here. It's so . . . ' I searched for the right word, 'so wild.'

'Yes, it is wild.' Her eyes shone. 'Wild. Untamed. Still free and powerful. Here nature remains untouched by all our so-called civilizations. And we are free here. You feel it too, I can tell.'

Thanis seemed ecstatic. This was a side of her I had never seen. I felt closer to her than ever before. She had shed her sophisticated, aloof image and become more open. I felt she was at one with the rocks and the sky and the wind that blew through her hair. It was almost as if she was part of the landscape, she seemed so at home here.

'Let's stay here,' I said. 'I want to draw it.'

'No, we have not arrived yet. We must go on,' she said firmly.

I was about to protest, but Thanis had already moved off. I was afraid she might leave me behind altogether, and I didn't want that. I shouted to her, 'Wait, slow down,' but she took no notice. She seemed to be going faster and faster, gliding over the rough ground with an animal's sureness of foot. I was trailing far behind.

When she reached the crest of the hill she finally paused. She turned and shouted, 'Come on, hurry up.'

This time I didn't bother to reply. I was going as fast as I could. The ground was much steeper here. Sometimes I had to climb over outcrops of stone or fight my way through dense thickets of gorse. The track, when I could see it, was slippy and I had to use my hands to stop myself falling.

But, finally, out of breath and feeling hot and bothered, I reached the top. In an instant everything was forgotten. One minute there had been nothing but the sky on the horizon, the next, there they were. A circle of standing stones. For some reason I counted them. Thirteen stones in all, most still perfectly upright, although one or two were leaning over away from the sea. I guessed they were about ten feet tall. When I finally came close I could see how weathered their surfaces were. I had to touch them. It was like having all of history under my finger tips. I was filled with a kind of madness and started to dance around them.

'I told you you would find inspiration here,' Thanis whispered. 'They are called the Wicca stones. No one knows why.'

'I can't believe it's so quiet here. We could be the only people in the whole world,' I said.

'Yes,' Thanis answered. 'It is always quiet here. There is no carpark, so the tourists don't come. And the locals stay away.'

'Why?' I asked. I found it hard to believe that you could stay away once you knew about this place.

'Wicca is an old word for witch. These are the witches' stones, Jessica. Most people are fools. They are too afraid to come here.' Thanis had lowered her voice. For some strange reason, it reminded me of the way people speak in church. Her tone seemed reverent, as if even she were slightly awed by the place.

'I had no idea there were stone circles in Cornwall. I know about Stonehenge, but I didn't know there were others,' I said.

Thanis sneered. 'There are many such places, but you have to know how to find them. They are all connected by hidden energies that run through the earth. I think you call them ley lines. In my language they have a different name.'

'Ley lines.' I repeated the word to myself. I had heard of them, but I had never really taken them seriously. I thought they were something for old hippies or new age travellers, not anything that ordinary people believed in. 'Do you really believe in them?' I asked.

'Of course I believe,' she said crossly. 'I can feel them, can't you? They are all around us. They meet in the centre of the circle. That is why the stones were placed here. This is a very powerful place. You can use that power if you know how. Open your mind, Jessica. You must free yourself from the modern world and all its restrictions. Don't hold yourself back. There is much I can teach you, but you must be ready to receive. I fear you are not ready yet.'

I wanted to ask her more questions, but Thanis had turned away from me. Had she told me such things in the city, I would not have believed her. Now, standing here, surrounded by the sky, sea, and miles of open countryside, I felt so isolated from the modern world that I no longer knew what to believe. But I knew I would come back here. I wanted to share in its magic. I wanted the rush of inspiration it gave me. Standing here, on land that had remained unchanged for thousands of years, I could feel something. Something unlike anything I had ever felt before. I felt recharged, as if I could achieve anything I wanted. It was a great way to feel.

I looked across at where Thanis was wandering around the hilltop, immersed in her own thoughts. I was sure she was feeling it too. I felt closer to her than ever before. Yet I was also a bit afraid of her. Things were happening so fast. I was travelling further and further away from the world I knew. Would I ever be able to find the way back?

20

It was getting dark when we made our way back to the village. We didn't talk much. I felt words could only spoil the experience we'd shared and to talk about anything else was impossible. All my senses were heightened, so even the lighted windows of the cottages we passed seemed magical. I couldn't believe that behind their curtains people would be watching TV or plugging in their electric kettles.

As we passed the mill I saw that Mel's lights were on.

'I think I'll just say hello to Mel,' I told Thanis. I wanted to make sure she was OK and also to share some of the things I was feeling. Thanis merely shrugged and walked off into the night.

'Mel, it's me,' I shouted as I knocked on the door.

'Jessica, what are you doing here? Is everything OK?'

'Yes, I'm fine. I was worried about you. I noticed the mill was all shut up earlier. Are you all right?' I asked.

'Just some trouble with the car. I broke down on the way to Penzance and had to wait ages for the garage to come and tow me in. It's such a nuisance. They say it'll take a week to get the spare parts. I'll have to get taxis everywhere.'

'I'm sorry,' I said. 'Maybe Thanis can give you a lift.'

'I'm not sure I trust her driving. She whizzed past me this morning, just before I broke down. I don't think she even noticed me.'

'She gets very impatient,' I replied.

'Just how much do you know about her?' Mel suddenly asked. 'Has she paid you yet.'

'No, but I'm not worried about that. She's a bit of a mystery, though. She doesn't like to talk about herself. I met this friend of hers. We went to his house yesterday,' I paused, not sure how much to tell her.

'And?'

'I had a bit of an accident myself. I'd climbed down to the beach and I found this secret cave . . . '

'There's lots of them around. You have to be careful, some of them go on for miles. They join up with the old tin mines,' Mel said. 'So what happened?'

'I'm not sure. I thought I heard voices, then I slipped and fell into this horrible, icy pool. I was sure I'd broken something, but Thanis and her friend appeared and pulled me out. She insists he's a healer.'

'And is he?' Mel asked earnestly.

'I don't know. My foot did stop hurting, so maybe he is. But I'm not sure. It might just have been the shock.'

'I don't want to scare you,' Mel said, 'but there have been rumours about that house. Your house, that is.'

'Oh, like what?'

'Remember I told you about all the cats? Well, they say that they only appear when that house is occupied. Apparently it lies empty for ages, then the owners turn up, stay a few months, and disappear again.'

'They travel a lot,' I said. 'I don't think that's very strange. I'd travel all the time too, if I had their money.'

'But how do they get their money?' Mel asked.

'Eva's a successful painter.'

'And Thanis?'

'Something to do with her family, I think. I don't know. We never talk about money.'

I wondered why Mel was looking at me so intently. 'Mel?'

'I'm sure this is just gossip, but the locals think she's a witch.' She rushed the words out.

'Thanis?'

'Eva. Probably Thanis too, I don't know. This is the first time the house has been occupied since we moved here. Don't look so worried. I'm sure it's just village gossip,' Mel said sympathetically.

'I hope so,' I said, thinking about those strangely powerful paintings that were piled up in the studio. 'It's probably just a coincidence, but do you know where Thanis took me today?'

'Where?' Mel asked. The atmosphere between us was charged with fear.

'The Wicca Stones.'

We stared at each other in horror, then simultaneously broke out in giggles.

'Listen to us,' Mel said. 'What a pair of gossips. I'm sure the gossip about me is just as bad. That's what comes of living in such a small village. I shouldn't have said anything. I'm sorry.'

'No, I'm glad you told me. I don't think Thanis would mind being called a witch anyway. She seems to believe in all kinds of weird and wonderful things. Luckily, I don't. She thinks I'm narrow minded.'

'Good for you,' Mel said. 'But, remember, my offer's still open. You can always come here. Anytime.'

'Thanks, but I'm sure I'll be fine. Anyhow, I think you should visit me next. I'd love to show you my work, and you can see Eva's paintings. Judge for yourself. That's if you're not too scared.' I smiled.

'Me? Scared? I'll have to come now, won't I? I can recognize a challenge when I hear one.'

21

Actually, Mel had scared me more than I'd let on. I really wanted to see how she'd respond to the paintings. I hadn't forgotten about the photographs I'd found either. There definitely was something strange about the house, but I wasn't ready to accept any supernatural explanations. Perhaps they did belong to some weird cult. Perhaps that was why the spiral was so important to them. But I didn't believe I was in any danger. Thanis had really looked after me. I felt like a proper artist now and I was grateful.

If I dreamed that night, I didn't remember anything about it when I woke up the next morning. At first I thought it was very early because it was so dark. But when I looked at my watch I saw it was already ten o'clock. I went over to the window and discovered that the outside world had disappeared in a thick mist. It swirled around the garden, giving just a hint here and there that the real world still existed. It was curiously depressing. I felt a longing for all the things I'd left behind in London. The busy streets, the traffic, the shops and cafés. Most of all, I was missing Jim. For the first time, I questioned whether I had made the right decision in coming here.

I got dressed quickly and crept downstairs. I wanted to get out of the house without seeing Thanis. I didn't want her to know I was phoning Jim, I'm not sure why. There was no sign of her anyhow. I had second thoughts when I opened the front door and the mist engulfed me. It was really strange outside. I could barely see the path under my feet and I hoped no cars would be coming down the narrow lane.

I wished I'd stopped to grab a raincoat as the air was so damp. My hair was dripping. I wasn't even sure where I was as it was so difficult to recognize anything. But the sound of the sea was louder now so I must be getting nearer the harbour. The wind was stronger here too. It blew the mist into weird shapes, making everything look sinister. Trees loomed over the road as if waiting to reach down and grab the unsuspecting traveller. At one point I was sure someone was lurking by the roadside, but it turned out to be only a roadsign. The mist seemed to taint all the air. I could feel it on my skin and taste it in my throat. I was glad no one else was around. I didn't want to see anyone or any thing emerging from it.

I quickened my pace. I felt as if I'd been walking for ages. I must be almost there. I was sure I'd just caught a glimpse of the phone box in front of me when I felt something brush against my leg. It was cold and damp and made me shudder. I remembered what Mel had told me about the wild cats. I was frightened. I looked down but could see nothing.

Had I imagined it? No, there it was again. What was it? I peered into the mist, but still couldn't see anything. Or rather, couldn't see anything I could recognize. Everywhere I looked there were dark shadows which seemed to be moving. Was it just a trick of the light? An illusion caused by the swirling mist and my own fear?

'Stop it!' I ordered myself. I was making it worse, giving in to panic.

I took some deep breaths. The fog tasted disgusting, but I felt a bit calmer. In a minute I could laugh about it, when I told Jim. What was that? Only a loose pebble tumbling down the road. There was another. It caught my ankle painfully. I looked around trying to get my bearings. That must be the sea. The phone box should be . . . There it was again. Something had dislodged a mass of small pebbles. I could hear them scattering over the surface.

Someone was out there. Someone or something. Were they trying to scare me? Or had I let my imagination run away with me? I wasn't taking any chances. I ran up onto the harbour wall, my arms out in front of me, desperately searching for the phone box door. At last. I flung myself inside and pulled the door to. My heart was pounding. The mist seemed to press against the glass, growing denser and denser. I leant against the door to hold it back. It still crept in through the cracks. I struggled to get my breath.

Eventually I realized it was quiet outside. Whoever it was had given up, unless they were waiting. I told myself not to be so ridiculous. I picked up the receiver and was relieved to hear the dialling tone. I felt in my pocket for the change I'd put there and began to dial Jim's number. It rang for ages.

'Come on, come on,' I said impatiently. 'Answer it. Please answer it.'

At last, the ringing stopped and Jim's mother answered, 'Yes, who is this?'

'Mrs Crosby, I must speak to Jim. It's urgent. I'm sorry . . .'

'He's not here,' she said crossly. 'Who is this?'

'I'm Jessica.'

'Oh, that girl from London. What do you want?'

'I want to speak to Jim. Please tell him,' I said coldly. I wasn't going to be put off by her rudeness.

'I've already told you he's not here. He's in hospital. He's had to have his leg reset. I knew that going to London would bring trouble.'

'What happened?' I asked. I had a horrible feeling in the pit of my stomach. I held on to the shelf for support. There was a disapproving silence at the other end of the line.

'The bone wasn't mending properly. It wasn't a clean break. They had to break it again and reset it.'

'But is he all right? It will heal, won't it?'

'What do you think? He's in a lot of pain. He might never get back to normal.' She sounded as if she might burst into tears.

'I'm so sorry. That's awful,' I said. 'Can I ring him at the hospital?'

'I'm sure he'll be in touch if he wants to,' she said shortly.

'I'd—' But she'd hung up.

I was shaking as I put the phone down. I'd had no idea Jim was in any danger. Why hadn't I rung him more often? What must he think of me? I would have visited him if I'd known. I'd really believed it was only a minor injury, that it was just a matter of time. He must be so depressed. I felt so guilty. I forgot all about my own problems. I pushed open the door of the phone box and stepped back out into the mist.

I heard a cat cry and looked down just in time to see it run across the path and jump down onto the beach. It was a large, sleek black cat. It turned to stare at me as it passed and I saw it held a small bird, still fluttering weakly, in its jaws. Any other time I might have tried to free it, but today I could do nothing. I looked away. I was too shocked. Should I go to him now? If the fog lifted

Thanis could drive me to the station. I felt depressed and helpless. I started to walk back to the house dejectedly. It would take hours to get to Liverpool, and what if Jim didn't want to see me?

22

My thoughts were as thick and muddled as the fog that swirled around me. I couldn't make sense of anything. I didn't know what to do. Part of me wanted to rush back to Jim, but another part didn't want to leave. A voice seemed to whisper in my ear, 'Don't be such a fool. Think of your future.' The worst thing was that voice didn't seem to be mine, even though it was inside my own head.

When I reached the house the front door was open. 'Thanis,' I shouted. There was no reply. The house didn't feel empty but it was strangely silent. I shouted again, louder this time. I felt sure someone was there. I closed the door and switched on the lights. The fog had invaded the house. I could see tendrils of it creeping across the floor and up the stairs. I had to get a grip on myself. My thoughts were going crazy.

Suddenly, I heard a floorboard creak above me. Thanis was here. I'd obviously just woken her up. I needed to talk to her. I rushed up the stairs and into her room. It was empty. 'Thanis,' I shouted. 'Where are you? I have to—' I swung around quickly, sure I'd heard a footstep behind me. 'Thanis,' I cried again, in a whisper this time. A shiver ran down my spine. All my senses told me something was watching me.

A strange scent seemed to pervade the room. An animal smell. I couldn't think what it reminded me of, but I knew I'd smelt it before. Was I going mad or was the room filling up with fog? I couldn't see properly. Wasn't that something moving in the corner of the room? Was something hiding in the fog? My eyes wouldn't focus properly. What was happening to me? I backed away. Something was there. It was between me and the door. I heard it hiss. Then, close to me, there was another sound. A cat began to cry and spit. The room seemed to come alive. An awful wailing had broken out. I felt sure something was circling around me. I could feel its cold, damp breath on my neck. It seemed to have sucked all the air out of the room. What was left was fetid, unbreathable.

I had to get out of there. I ran to the door and pulled it shut behind me. The noise stopped immediately. I shuddered. I started towards the stairs. I tried to tell myself I'd overreacted. My imagination had gone out of control. My rational mind rejected what had happened. It insisted there was no mystery. There was always a reason for everything. One of the stray cats had got into the house when Thanis had left the door open. I'd have to go up and let it out later. When I'd calmed down. When the fog had lifted. But it wasn't so easy to free myself from the feeling of dread that gripped me. Too much was happening. I couldn't make sense of it.

I was halfway down the stairs when I heard a movement outside. Suddenly someone was banging on the door. The noise filled the house with menace. I felt all my fear rush back. I forced myself to move forward. I had to get control. I took a deep breath and opened the door.

23

'Mel, I'm so glad it's you.'

'Jessica, what's wrong? You look as if you've just seen a ghost.' Mel stood on the doorstep rubbing her fingers through her damp hair. She looked small and vulnerable with the fog looming around her.

'It's nothing,' I said. 'Come in. Isn't this weather spooky? It's just made me a bit jumpy.'

I led the way into the large living room and switched on the lights.

'This is amazing,' Mel said, raising her eyebrows. 'I love the colours.'

'It surprised me too. The house is full of surprises,' I said.

'So where's your studio? I can't wait to see it.' Mel was enthusiastic. That was one of the things I really liked about her. Just having her here made everything seem normal again.

'I'll make coffee first, then we'll go upstairs. I'm dying to hear what you think of my work.' I was, but I wasn't ready to go back up there yet. I needed more time to pull myself together.

I took my time making the coffee. If Mel noticed anything wrong she didn't say anything. Half an hour later we climbed the stairs and headed for the door that led to the attic. I was listening intently as we passed Thanis's door, but I couldn't hear a thing.

'It's cold up here,' Mel said shivering. 'It's even worse than the mill. Someone should fix the windows. Look at the fog getting in.'

We went up the narrow wooden stairs into the studio. I went to get the spiral nervously. Mel would be the first person to judge my work, and I really cared about her opinion. She held it carefully in her fingers and looked at it in silence. I waited anxiously.

'It's lovely, Jessica,' she said at last, smiling. 'It's so delicate.'

'Really? You're not just being polite?' I asked.

'And why would I be polite? That's far too English for me. It's very unusual. Where did you get the idea?'

'It wasn't mine. Thanis showed me what she wanted. It has some family significance.' I took the spiral from her and put it back carefully in its box.

'Where is she anyhow?' Mel asked.

'I've no idea. I never know where she is or what she does all day.'

'And you're OK with that? I mean, I'm sure she's . . .' Mel fumbled for the right word. 'Maybe she's just eccentric, but you are all alone with her here. Doesn't that worry you?'

'No,' I said. 'Why should it?' I started to sort through my sketches. I didn't want to talk about Thanis.

'You're hiding something from me,' Mel said determinedly. 'Go on. What is it? Has something happened?'

'No. Not exactly. The truth is I'm not sure. I thought I heard something, then it was so foggy. I don't know. I suppose it was just a cat.' Maybe it would be a relief to tell someone.

'What was? You can trust me,' Mel encouraged.

I decided I would trust her. I needed to talk to someone. I told her everything that had happened that morning.

'I suppose Thanis had left the window open. That would explain the fog and the cat,' I finished hopefully.

'There's only one way to find out. Come on.' Mel didn't wait for an answer. She was already at the top of the stairs. By the time we reached Thanis's door we were both giggling.

'It's like being back at school,' Mel whispered. 'Go on. Open the door.'

I turned the handle and pushed the door open before I had time to change my mind. We both fell silent. There was still a definite smell in the room, different to the rest of the house. I looked up at the window. It was closed. I went over to check the catch, but it was firmly secured. There was no way the window could have blown open.

'Look at this,' Mel whispered. I turned around to see her standing by a cupboard that was fitted into the wall. I couldn't see what she was looking at, until she slowly backed away, throwing wide the doors as she did so. I could hardly believe my eyes. Mel grabbed my hand and we stood dumbfounded for a minute or two. Mel had found the source of the smell. It was a cat. But not any cat that had prowled the lanes of Cornwall. This cat hadn't walked anywhere. Not for at least two thousand years.

24

'That's creepy,' Mel said, when we were safely back in the living room. 'You can't stay here. Move in with me. Jack won't be back for ages.'

'It's a bit spooky, yes. But it might not mean anything. It might not even be hers,' I suggested.

'A bit spooky. You're crazy. We find a mummified cat in a cupboard and you're making excuses. It stinks. No normal person could sleep in that room. And—' Mel stopped suddenly. The atmosphere went cold.

'What is it? Mel, you're scaring me.' I waited for her to speak.

'You thought there was a cat in the room, didn't you?'

70

'Yes,' I said doubtfully.

'You heard it move?'

'I thought I heard something move.'

'And you heard it cry.' Mel looked at me meaningfully. She continued, 'And we did find a—'

'No,' I said firmly. 'Absolutely no way. I refuse to believe a mummified cat was walking around that room this morning. Maybe I heard a cat in the garden, or maybe I imagined it, but I definitely, definitely didn't see anything as crazy as that.'

'Then ask her,' Mel said crossly. 'Ask her what it's doing there.'

'I can't. How can I? What could I say? By the way, Thanis, we just happened to look in your cupboard and . . . '

'OK. Maybe that wasn't such a good idea. Maybe the best thing is just to pack your bags and get out of here now,' Mel said.

'No,' I said, shaking my head. 'You're trying to scare me. I can't leave now. I won't give my work up.'

'You can't spend another night here. Stay at my place. Make up an excuse. Tell her anything. You can still finish your work.' Mel sounded urgent.

I shook my head. 'I'll be finished soon. I'll be leaving then anyhow. Thanis wouldn't hurt me, I'm sure of that.'

'You can't be sure of anything. Why did she invite you here in the first place? Didn't you ever ask yourself that? Cornwall's full of artists. Why you?'

'And why not me?' I shouted. 'I'm an artist too. She wanted me.'

'I didn't mean it like that.' Mel paused. 'Jessica, listen to me. You don't know what you're getting yourself into. There's something weird about this house. Everyone knows it.'

We were both shouting so much neither of us heard the door opening. A sudden draught made me look up and there was Thanis standing in the doorway. Her eyes glanced around the room and narrowed as they settled on Mel.

71

'I see we both have visitors today,' Thanis said in her slow, precise English.

I realized I could hear voices coming from the hallway.

'I have a surprise for you, Jessica,' she said. 'Let me introduce Eva and Peter.'

25

'Eva, Peter,' I said weakly as they came over and shook my hand. They ignored Mel completely. She rose awkwardly and said she had to be going. I noticed how pale she looked, so unlike her usual self.

'I hear your work is going well,' Eva said, as she settled herself on the sofa. Her perfume was so overpowering I felt myself draw back. She flicked her hair from her cheeks and turned pale, watery blue eyes on me. She seemed weary, as if nothing in the world was of interest to her. Her bored expression was out of tune with the rather dramatic way she dressed. She wore a black trouser suit and high heeled shoes that were totally unsuited to the rough surfaces of the local lanes. When she unbuttoned her jacket I saw the heavy pendant hanging around her neck. It was the same mysterious symbol that Thanis had given me, only much larger. She was very glamorous. I took an instant dislike to her. I felt sure she didn't like me either.

'Go and get the spiral,' Thanis ordered, prodding me in the arm.

'They won't—' I began to say but Thanis cut me off brusquely.

'Go. Don't argue,' she said.

I did as I was told, but I wasn't happy. I climbed the stairs slowly, dragging my feet. I wasn't ready for this. It was too soon. Too unexpected. What if they didn't like it? What if I'd failed? But that wasn't the only thing bothering me as I opened the door to the studio. I knew that underneath was something else.

I felt like an intruder. It was no longer my studio. It was hers. It was over. I felt as though I'd been living in a dream and now I'd been woken up. I didn't want it to end. Not so soon. Not without any warning. I realized I wasn't ready to go back to London and my old life.

I picked up the spiral angrily and slammed the door behind me. I wanted it to be my studio. I couldn't bear the thought of Eva in there. Not now I'd finally met her. Why couldn't she have waited another week? Then my work would have been finished. I might have been ready to move on. I would have been prepared.

As I re-entered the living room something stopped me in my tracks. I hesitated on the threshold, unable to stop myself staring. They all sat in a row on the sofa, waiting. They weren't talking or laughing. They just sat perfectly still. That was how I saw it. The resemblance to the photographs. The ones I'd found in their room upstairs. Take away the modern haircuts and the fashionable clothing and you'd think it was the same people. Only now they weren't looking at the camera. They were looking straight at me.

26

'Yes,' Eva sighed. 'It's almost finished. Soon it will be over.'
She passed the spiral back to Thanis. I couldn't understand
why she looked so relieved.

'You have done well,' Peter said. 'This is exactly what we
need.'

'I told you she was the one,' Thanis said. 'There was no
need to worry.'

Peter shrugged. 'Do the others know?' he asked. Thanis
shook her head.

'What others?' I wanted to know.

'Only Nuskhet and one or two friends. People from the
old country. You need not concern yourself,' Thanis told
me.

'But why not? You see, we are all concerned with your
work,' Eva said smiling defiantly. Thanis threw her a
warning look. 'You can have no idea how much this little
spiral means to us,' she went on. 'I'm sure Thanis has not
told you everything. She never does.'

'I'm lost,' I said. 'I've no idea what you are talking about.'
I picked up the spiral and turned away. I had no intention of
letting Eva come between me and Thanis. I didn't trust her
one bit.

'Take no notice of her,' Thanis shouted after me as I left
the room.

I didn't go back to the studio. I sat in my bedroom and
stared down into the garden. I wanted to talk to Mel, to try
and get everything into some kind of perspective. But I
hadn't forgotten our argument yet. It was too soon. I'd walk
up to the mill later. I didn't like Eva, but maybe she would
solve the mystery of Thanis. She might know the answers to

the questions that had been troubling me. If I knew more about her I'd be able to put Mel's mind at rest. I decided I'd talk to Eva as soon as I got the chance.

27

I passed a troubled night. The strange events of the previous day were rushing round and round in my mind. Only everything was all mixed up. I could hear Mel's voice calling me, but I couldn't find her anywhere. I opened lots of doors. Behind them was always Eva. Mel's voice became fainter and fainter. I was still deep in dreams when I heard the banging. I was lost in the darkness, unable to find my way back. At first I thought I was hearing my heartbeat, then it became more and more frantic. I awoke with a struggle, my eyes still heavy with sleep. It was barely light yet someone was hammering on the door.

I got out of bed unwillingly, pulled on my jeans and sweater and staggered down the stairs to the front door. The banging hadn't stopped. I wondered where everyone was. They couldn't be sleeping through all this noise. I opened the door with a feeling of dread.

'Jessica, thank God it's you.'

'Mel, what's the matter? What's happened?' I asked, leaning on the door for support.

Mel stood shivering on the doorstep. Her normally spiky hair hung limp and damp around her forehead. I took her arm and tried to help her into the living room. She shook her head.

'No,' she said. 'I can't. You have to come with me.' She burst into tears.

'What is it? Tell me.' I had to force the words out.

'I couldn't look,' she whispered. 'Not on my own.' I waited for her to go on. 'They got my birds. All of them.'

'What happened?' I asked.

'I went out to feed them as usual. At first I didn't notice anything. Then I realized it was too quiet. Something was wrong.' Mel paused. She wasn't looking at me. Her eyes were still seeing whatever she'd seen then. 'I went to the hen house. I always put them in there at night, because of the foxes.' Now she turned her eyes to me. They filled with tears. 'It was empty. They're all gone. You have to come with me. I know something's happened to them. I'm sure of it.'

'Of course I'll come,' I told her. 'We'll find them. Maybe they're OK.' Even as I said it, I knew that wasn't true. A feeling of dread had settled in my stomach. Mel didn't reply. I don't think she heard anything I said. I reached over and touched her arm.

'Come on,' I said. 'Let's get it over with.'

I left her on the doorstep while I grabbed a jacket and my sandals. Then we hurried up the lane to her house. The fog had begun to lift and we could see a few feet in front of us. It was still spooky. We held onto each other's arm. Neither of us had any hope. I was thinking of the first day I'd visited the mill. How peaceful it had been. How idyllic it had seemed. That was only ten days ago, but it felt more like an age. I even felt a bit responsible. As if I'd brought her bad luck. But that was ridiculous. Things happened in the country. That was nature. Everything ate everything else.

When we got there the garden was unnaturally quiet. Our feet on the gravel drive were the only sound. No birds sang. No traffic sounded in the distance.

'Shall we separate?' I whispered. Mel shook her head and fastened her grip on my arm.

'This way,' she said.

We left the drive and walked over the damp grass to the hen house. I looked at the door. It had been pulled off its hinges. No fox had done that. My feeling of dread deepened. I looked around the empty enclosure fearing what we might find. There were a few feathers scattered around but no sign of anything unusual.

Mel's face was drained of colour as she led me back out into the garden. I followed her down to the stream. Everything looked so pretty. The flowers emerging from the mist, their petals heavy with moisture. The clear water flowing over the pebbles in the stream. That made it all so much worse. Mel's cries. The torn and bloody bodies. Some still fluttering feebly. The feathers floating everywhere as beautiful as snow.

28

I stayed with Mel while she phoned the police and the vet. They arrived an hour later, but there wasn't much they could do. When they'd finished I helped her collect the bodies and bury them in the woods at the bottom of her garden. She was still drained of colour. She moved with a mechanical precision as if in a trance.

'Someone hates me,' she said.

'No,' I reassured her. 'You heard what the police said. It's vandals. You're not the only one it's happened to.'

Mel's eyes gazed blankly at me. 'I heard nothing. Why didn't I wake up? My beautiful birds. All gone. All of them.' She shook her head as if she could shake off the memory of what we'd found. I knew she wouldn't succeed. I still saw it myself. 'What kind of person could do it?' she asked.

'I don't know. Only a very sick one—' I stopped. I felt overwhelmed by all the things that were happening. Had the world gone mad? It all seemed like a bad dream.

'What will you do?' I asked.

Mel shrugged. She was slumped in an old armchair in her studio. I handed her another mug of coffee and pulled a chair over to sit facing her.

'Don't worry,' I told her. 'I'll sort something out. You can't stay here.'

'No,' Mel said slowly. 'Not now.'

We drank our coffee in silence. I had my own decisions to make. Maybe it was time for me to leave too. The summer was almost over. My work here would be finished in another day or two.

Suddenly I wanted to get away. I knew what I had to do.

I rang directory enquiries and got the phone number of all the hospitals in Liverpool. Luckily, Jim was in the second one I rang. I spoke to the sister in charge and gave her Mel's number. I waited impatiently for the phone to ring.

'Jim,' I said eagerly, as I picked it up. 'Are you OK? I just spoke to your mother yesterday. I had no idea . . . '

'I'll survive,' he replied. His voice sounded cold and distant.

'How are you?' I asked, trying to sound as if I hadn't noticed. 'What happened? Your mother wouldn't tell me much.'

'No? She thinks you're . . . bad luck.' He'd hesitated over the words. I was appalled. I wished he hadn't said them. He went on, 'She thinks if I'd just stayed in Liverpool it wouldn't have happened.' I felt a cold shiver run down my spine. I didn't know what to say. 'I told her she's crazy, but you know how mothers are,' he continued. 'Jessica, you still there?'

'Yes I'm here. I . . . ' I hesitated. What could I tell him? I didn't understand what was happening myself. 'I'm sorry,' I said.

'For what? I'm not blaming you for anything,' Jim reassured me.

'No, I know, but . . . I should have rung you before. I've just been so involved in my work and . . . ' I regretted saying that immediately.

'Forget it,' Jim said. 'I know your work means everything to you.'

There was an awkward silence. 'I didn't mean it like that,' I said finally. 'I wish you were here. Really. I miss you.'

'Look,' Jim told me. 'I can't talk now. The doctors are just coming round. I'll see you soon. It's almost September. We'll talk then, OK?'

'Yes. I'll see you back at college. Jim, I—' A horrible feeling swept over me as the line went dead.

29

I walked back to the house slowly. I felt so alone and miserable. The mill was all locked up. Mel had gone to stay with her husband in Bristol for a few days. The fog had finally cleared and it was a beautiful day. But that didn't help me. I still felt shocked and confused. Deep down, I feared I had brought bad luck to everyone.

When I got back Thanis was in the kitchen. She seemed in an unusually good mood.

'Enjoy your walk?' she asked, smiling. Her eyes were bright and full of life.

'No. Not exactly.' I told her what had happened to Mel.

'How terrible,' she said. She was still smiling.

'Mel's in a terrible state,' I said reproachfully.

'Is she? Well, I'm sure she'll get over it. They're only birds. She can buy more,' Thanis said casually as she switched on the kettle. 'By the way, were you in my room yesterday?'

'Yes, I thought one of the stray cats had got in.' I watched her warily to see how she reacted. 'I heard something.'

'You should be careful, Jessica. They are wild. Not your usual pets.'

'There seems to be an awful lot of them around. Have you noticed?' I asked.

'It's such a perfect place for them. It's so much better to be wild and free, don't you agree? You would scare it, shutting it in like that.'

'It scared me,' I said.

'Really, Jessica, there's no reason for you to be scared. Now, I think we have wasted enough time today. Have you given up work?'

'No. I'm almost finished.'

'Good. Because I want the spiral for tonight. You must be ready.'

'Tonight?' I was shocked. 'Why tonight?'

'Because it is time,' she said enigmatically.

'Time for what?' I asked.

'Time for you to get to work. You will know everything this evening. I promise you. I know you won't let me down,' Thanis said quietly.

'No, of course not,' I replied, although I still wasn't sure what we were talking about.

30

I put everything out of my mind and got to work putting the finishing touches to the spiral. I polished the silver until it shone. It was a relief to lose myself in my work. This was the one thing that hadn't gone wrong. I was determined not to spoil it now. I wouldn't let anything interfere with my work. There was nothing I could do for Mel or Jim. But I was in control of my own destiny. This was my chance. I had to make the most of it.

I worked all afternoon until the spiral was finished. I knew there was nothing more I could do to it. I was pleased with the result, but I also felt sad. I'd have to hand it over. It wouldn't be mine any more. I held it up to the light. There was something very satisfying about the shape. I was proud of it. And tonight Thanis had promised to tell me everything. She trusted me. I hadn't brought her bad luck.

I decided to take a last look at the paintings piled up against the studio walls. Now I'd met Eva they seemed more of a puzzle than ever. It was hard to connect these dark, passionate landscapes with the world-weary woman who'd arrived so unexpectedly yesterday. There was something forbidding about them. I thought of the rumours Mel had told me and shuddered. Could Eva really be a witch? Was that the strange power I felt in these paintings? And what about Thanis? And Nuskhet? Was that why they were drawn to wild, deserted places?

No. It was all too impossible. I put the paintings back carefully where I'd found them. People change. Artists change their style. There had to be a more ordinary explanation. I began to tidy up the studio. I removed all my sketches and equipment and put them in my bedroom. The studio was Eva's now. I said goodbye silently and gave it a long, last look before I closed the door for the final time.

It was early evening before I came downstairs. When I entered the living room the scene seemed so normal any lingering doubts fled. The coffee table was covered with packages from a shopping trip to Penzance. Eva sat painting her nails while Thanis flicked through a magazine. Peter was in the kitchen peeling a large bowl of potatoes.

'We'll never eat all those,' I said as I went in to make coffee.

'We're expecting guests,' he said. 'Didn't Thanis tell you?'

Immediately, all my doubts raced back. There was an awkward silence while I went through the motions of filling my cup with boiling water and stirring in the milk. I could feel Peter's eyes watching me. I was shocked. Why hadn't Thanis told me? Who were these guests? Were they the 'others' Eva had talked about?

'I expect she wanted to surprise you,' Peter said at last, as if he'd read my mind. 'This is a celebration.'

'A celebration?' I repeated, feeling the shock recede.

'Of your work, of course. We always have a celebration when a new work is finished. We want you to know how much we appreciate what you have done for us,' Peter said, wiping his hands on a tea towel. 'I'm glad you've been able to work here.'

'Yes,' I said. 'My work has gone well.'

'You are at the beginning, Jessica. Enjoy it. Success will not always be so sweet.'

31

A little later Peter and Thanis decided to go for a walk, leaving Eva and me to finish preparing the meal. I had the feeling they had something they wanted to discuss in private. I hoped it might be about me. If Peter could be persuaded to represent my work, my career might really take off. He had so many contacts, and all over the world too.

As I entered the kitchen Eva was already heating olive oil in a pan. She didn't smile or greet me and I wondered if she had minded me staying in her house and using her studio. She seemed ill at ease. I said the first thing that came into my mind.

'Have you known Thanis long?'

'Since I was very young,' she sighed. 'I met Peter through her.'

A look of sadness crossed her face. Perhaps they weren't so close as I'd imagined.

'Before you were an artist?' I asked.

'Before everything,' she said with a wry smile, throwing some spices into the pan.

'But you always knew you would be an artist?'

'Oh yes. I thought art was everything.'

'Well, it is, isn't it?' I joked, trying to lighten the atmosphere.

She swung around to face me and said seriously, 'No, it is not. Do not make that mistake, Jessica. You are so young. All your life is before you. Art is important; maybe, art is wonderful sometimes, but it is not everything.'

I lowered my eyes. I was embarrassed. She was so touchy, no subject seemed safe. I wished the others would return. There was an awkward silence while I searched unsuccessfully for a safe topic of conversation. Eva chopped vegetables with a surprising speed and handed me the rice to wash.

'I don't mean to be unkind,' she said at last. 'Take no notice of me. I'm too old, too jaded. Once I had your enthusiasm.'

'You're not old,' I protested. She brushed me aside.

'You know nothing, you fool,' she said crossly. 'I'm wasting my breath. I'm trying to help you.'

'Help me?' I said disbelievingly. I was angry now. I knew she was trying to discourage me.

'No,' she replied sadly. 'You don't understand, how could you?'

We were both silent for some minutes and I thought the conversation was over until she unexpectedly continued, 'There are always choices to be made in life, sometimes more than you realize. What I am trying to say is that you must choose carefully.'

'I've always wanted to be an artist,' I said seriously. 'It's all I've ever wanted.'

'Ah well.' She shrugged. 'Then I'm sure you will have success.'

I think she regretted her bad temper because for the next half hour she entertained me with tales of the different galleries she'd exhibited in. She'd travelled everywhere, Paris, New York, Berlin, Milan. No wonder she seemed so sophisticated, so cosmopolitan. It was hard to believe this was the woman who'd painted those dark, stormy landscapes. There was obviously more to Eva than met the eye, but I wasn't sure I wanted to find out more. I didn't like her. She'd tried to treat me like a child. As if I didn't already know what I wanted out of life.

Well, I didn't have to like her. I'd be free to leave tomorrow. I could forget about all of them if I wanted to. Only I didn't want to. I wanted to know more about them.

'Tell me about Thanis,' I said.

'I wish I could,' she replied.

'But you've known her for years,' I said reproachfully.

'You have to ask her yourself, Jessica. You'll get your chance tonight. Now you should go and get ready. You want to make an impression. This will be an important night for you.'

32

I showered and changed into my one smart dress. The house seemed strangely quiet. I wondered why the guests hadn't arrived yet. I wasn't even sure if Thanis and Peter had returned from their walk. I had mixed feelings about the evening ahead. If it was just a few old friends, then why all the mystery? And why hadn't I met any of them before now? I was sure they were keeping something from me. Had they some surprise planned? Maybe another commission?

I spent ages putting my make up on. I didn't want to look unsophisticated next to Eva. After all, in a way this was my party. I couldn't decide what jewellery to wear. In the end I fastened the gold rune around my neck thinking it would please Thanis. I looked at myself in the bathroom mirror. I looked different. The weeks I'd spent here had changed me. Was this a face that could take the art world by storm? I decided it was. I went downstairs with a new confidence in my step. I'd done it. I was a success. The future would be mine.

The house seemed deserted. I could smell food cooking in the kitchen but no one was there. In the living room a long table had been set up. I counted the number of places. There were thirteen. Glass and silver gleamed in the late evening sun. All around the room were candles waiting to be lit. Why were there no guests? Where was everybody?

I soon got bored with waiting. I grabbed my jacket and walked down to the harbour. I sat on the wall and watched the waves breaking gently on the shore. I was filled with a sense of anticipation. I remembered the evening I'd first arrived. Now all the dreams I'd had then seemed about to come true. I watched the sun set and disappear behind the horizon. I was ready. Whatever happened tonight, I was prepared.

33

'Jessica, perfect timing,' Thanis said when I entered the living room. 'Let me introduce you to everyone.' She took my arm and led me around the room. I was glad I was looking my best. The men and women around me were all dressed smartly, but in a strangely dated style. The women wore too much make up and jewellery. The men looked stiff and uncomfortable in their formal suits.

'My dear, so pleased to be here,' Nuskhet told me as he shook my hand. He was leaning heavily on a strong stick that was topped by a gold lion's head. His head seemed uncertainly perched on his shoulders and shook almost imperceptibly as he spoke. 'Let me introduce my nieces Neret and Iaret.' Two women nodded to me, without standing up. 'They are saving their strength,' Nuskhet told me. 'Over there, you will see their husbands. And this is my great-granddaughter Kara, the beauty of the family.'

Kara smiled at me warmly. She had enormous almond-shaped eyes fringed by heavy lashes. 'I'm sure we'll be good friends,' she whispered. 'We'll have time to talk later.'

'Are they all your family?' I asked Nuskhet.

'Mostly, yes. We were once much greater than you see now.'

'And Thanis? Is she a relation?'

'Ah no, not Thanis. She is one of a kind, as I think your people say. Now, you must excuse these ancient limbs. Age is such a burden. The aches, the pains, the weakness,' Nuskhet said, looking around for a chair.

'Shall we eat?' Peter said walking in from the kitchen. 'You know where you must sit. Jessica, you should be here, in the place of honour.'

I was placed at the top of the table, with my back to the window. Eva and Peter were to each side. Eva looked as out of place as I did. She was wearing a velvet trouser suit over a daringly low cut halter necked top. Her pale gold hair was swept up in a French pleat.

'You're not wearing your pendant?' Thanis said quietly. 'I think you have forgotten it.'

'No,' Eva replied, deliberately not looking at her. 'And you know why.'

Thanis looked furious. I had never seen her struggle to control herself before. For a moment she reminded me of a wild animal about to strike. Then she shrugged, whispering something under her breath.

'So, what does it matter now. Tonight we are celebrating the new artist, not the old,' Thanis said pointedly. She looked around the table and everyone fell silent. 'A toast, to Jessica,' she commanded raising her wine glass, 'and to the new life she will bring us.'

I smiled. I was exalting in my triumph over Eva. I was surprised when she joined in the toast. 'Yes, to Jessica, to her success and my freedom.' She lowered her voice and whispered to me, 'You don't know how long I have waited for this night.'

'I want to thank you for everything,' I said to Thanis. 'You've done so much for me. But I'd like to understand. Why is the spiral so important to you? You promised you'd tell me everything tonight.'

I saw Nuskhet nod to Thanis who said, 'Yes, it is time. You see, we are the last remnants of a once powerful civilization. So old, even the history books have forgotten us. We have passed on our culture and our traditions through generation after generation. We have suffered persecution and exile. Now we keep to ourselves. We do not share our secrets with strangers. We have learned to be cautious.'

I looked around the table. Everyone had stopped eating and waited in silence for Thanis to continue. Only Eva raised her glass and continued to drink. 'Tell her about the spiral,' she said.

'The spiral. Of course. You see, Jessica, when you found the rune that day in the museum I knew you were the chosen one. For us, art is not just something you buy and sell. It is much, much more. The symbol is the life. It gives us our strength. But it does not last forever. It loses its power and needs to be replaced. Each age must have its own symbol. The rune, which you wear around your neck, belongs to the past. It is finished. Your spiral will give us our future.' She paused. 'And, of course, your own. We will not forget what you have done for us.'

'Yes,' Peter said solemnly, 'you are one of us now. We will protect you too.'

I wondered at his choice of words. 'I don't understand,' I said. 'How can a spiral give you strength? What does it mean?'

'Always so many questions. Your age is in such a hurry to know everything, yet it is too stupid to understand the answers,' Thanis said, picking up her fork and beginning to eat again.

'Thanis, as you can see, does not understand the world we live in,' Eva said loudly. 'She talks of the future but she prefers to live in the past. Are you sure you're ready to give up the world? Do you really want to become one with them?'

'You know what I want,' I said, determined not to let her spoil my evening. 'I want to be an artist. I want success.'

'You will have success, Jessica. There is no doubt of that,' Thanis said.

I had more questions I wanted to ask, but I decided to wait till later, when I could speak to her alone. No one spoke much as we finished the meal. Occasionally someone whispered something to a neighbour and I would feel their eyes turn to me. But when I looked up they always turned away quickly.

After the main course was finished, Kara cleared the plates while two of the other women made coffee. Someone carried in a tray of fruit and a dish of sweets made with nuts and syrup. The candles had burned low. The room suddenly seemed unbearably stuffy. I went over to open the window and stood for a moment enjoying the draught of fresh air.

The moon was so bright everything in the garden was illuminated with a weird, greenish glow. It was as if the trees and flowers were dark counterparts of their normal, daytime selves. The woods seemed to have crept closer to the house. I felt afraid of the utter darkness that waited there. The whole world was strangely still. I felt as if time had stopped. I feared we would be lost in this moment for ever, that somehow we'd fallen out of time. I thought of what Thanis had said about the spiral. Could it really have some sort of power over the future?

No, I mustn't get caught up in their crazy ideas. I believed in the modern world. I'd shut out the moon and the night. I reached up to pull the curtain across the window. Suddenly, I caught sight of the reflection of Thanis and some of the others in the glass. They too looked different somehow.

Their dark eyes seemed to merge into the blackness of the sky. They'd lost that stiff formality that had characterized the people I'd just shared a meal with. They didn't look so tired. They seemed full of life, alert. They even looked younger. Was that really Nuskhet moving towards me?

I turned round quickly. The smile froze on my lips. Everyone was different. What was going on? Why was everyone getting to their feet? Why were they all moving towards me?

34

Nothing was making sense. As if in sympathy with my distress, somewhere in the night a cat began to howl. Not far away others answered. 'What is it?' I asked, looking desperately from one to another of them. 'Is something wrong?'

'Wrong?' Thanis laughed. 'No, nothing is wrong. We are impatient. We are tired of waiting. We are waiting for you, Jessica.'

I was lost for words. I saw Thanis's lips move, but it was not her voice. Gone was the careful English. This voice was deeper and more heavily accented. Her words echoed around my head. My mind went blank. I began to feel strangely calm.

'Come, Jessica, join us,' she said, smiling seductively. She held out her hand to me and I found myself moving slowly towards her. Nothing seemed real. Everything was happening in slow motion. I knew I must be dreaming. 'You have nothing to fear, come,' she repeated.

I hesitated. Why were the others all watching me like that? Why were they closing around me in a circle? Suddenly my mind filled with all the rumours I'd heard about this house, about Eva and Thanis. About the plague of stray cats. There'd been other things too. I struggled to remember. My brain seemed paralysed. I couldn't think straight.

'Join us,' Neret and Iaret appealed. They were stretching long, bony fingers towards me. I tried to back away but I couldn't move. I felt their cold hands taking hold of mine. 'You belong with us. Don't fight us,' they whispered, one in each ear. I could no longer tell if their voices were outside or inside my head.

I pulled my hands free and covered my ears. 'No,' I whispered, but the voices wouldn't go away. They were spinning round my head. Making me dizzy. Everything was all mixed up. Why could I hear cats? Had someone let the cats in? I couldn't stand any more. I was going mad.

'That is enough,' a man commanded. I turned my head with an enormous effort. It was Nuskhet. His skin was still as lined as ever, but he stood so straight he towered over the others. All except Thanis who stood by his side. 'It is time. You must choose,' he said firmly.

'Yes,' Thanis agreed. 'It is your choice. You have given us what we need. Now we can give you what you most desire. Why are you so afraid? Do you really want to return to your old life? To be a nobody? To live always with regrets.'

I hesitated. 'I've my art, my talent. I'll succeed. I don't need you,' I insisted.

'You think you will be content to struggle with your drawings like before? No, Jessica. Once you have felt the power you cannot give it up. Do not be afraid. We will not harm you. Do not fight us. You are one with us. Trust me.' Once again, she held out her hand in invitation.

I shook my head. I opened my mouth to tell her no, never. I was determined not to give in. Then I found myself gazing up at the stars. I saw the beauty of the night sky, of the darkness that was waiting outside. All my fears evaporated. I went forward to join them.

35

I followed Thanis to the door. As I stepped out into the night garden they each came up and kissed me on the cheeks. Their lips felt dry and light as tissue paper. Their breath seemed feeble. I looked around in a daze. 'Come, we must hurry,' Thanis said kindly. She threw off the shawl she'd been wearing round her shoulders. I saw she was wearing the spiral, hanging from a choker of twisted silk. Her hair flowed down her back, darker than the night around us. She was wearing a long red dress which fell in gentle pleats around her ankles. Her feet seemed to be bare. Was she real or an apparition? Would she vanish without warning? I expected to wake up at any moment.

I wasn't left to my thoughts for long. Eva prodded me in the back and pushed me forwards. I tried to catch her eye but she wouldn't look directly at me. Thanis led the way through the garden. We crossed the stream one by one and entered the dark woods. We walked in single file. I was aware of my legs moving but I couldn't feel the earth under my feet. I could swear I saw the trees parting before us, as a crowd parts for a queen.

The night was perfectly still. No one spoke. There wasn't a breath of wind. No leaf shivered as we passed. No bird shrieked in alarm. I'd never known such utter silence. Above us the moon was at its height. A thousand stars shone in the dark sky. This was a reality I'd never even glimpsed before. Now I was a part of it. It was exhilarating. There was an air of expectancy as if the whole world was waiting. And I was waiting too.

I lost all sense of time. I don't know how long we'd walked before we came out of the woods on to the moor. I could see outcrops of granite rising around us like grotesque sculptures. But they weren't inanimate any more. I could feel the life pulsing through them. There was life everywhere. In the earth, the stones, the few stunted trees that were outlined against the sky.

Thanis turned back and, taking me to one side, whispered, 'Soon you will see, I told you there was power in this place. Look around you. Open your eyes.'

'I am looking,' I said.

'No, you are not seeing yet. You must be willing to see or I cannot help you.'

What did she mean? I was looking. I began to feel angry. What more did she want of me?

'Try harder, Jessica. Do not disappoint me,' her voice commanded. 'You want to be a great artist, then you must try.'

I shut my eyes to try and refocus them. When I opened them again I finally saw what she meant. I looked around in amazement. This was a whole new landscape. There were lines of power everywhere. They were all around me, crisscrossing the earth in one giant network of energies. Instead of hills and rocky outcrops I saw peaks of brightness and pools of darkness.

'This is awesome,' I stuttered. 'What is it?'

'This is the power I promised you, Jessica. These are the earth's energies. Here the power is still strong. See how the energies flow freely as they have done since ancient times. Listen, can you hear the earth singing?'

'Yes,' I said ecstatically. 'I can hear something.'

'Everything has its voice,' she said. 'The earth calls to the sky. The rocks call to the sea. Even the water that trickles through the earth has its own unique song for those who choose to hear.'

'I can hear it,' I said enthusiastically. 'I can hear it.'

'Your world has destroyed so much. All you have done with your science is pollute and damage the earth. Even the skies have been violated. My culture is very different. We respect nature. We worship her forces. In return, she gives us her power. Now you will share that power. There is much to teach you. You will not regret your choice.'

By now the others were no longer in sight. We hurried after them. Everything seemed so effortless.

'Where are we going?' I asked.

'To the Stones. Where else?'

36

By some trick of the moon the Wicca Stones looked much taller than they had in daylight. Their shadows reached out to us, as if drawing us in to their centre.

'Follow me,' Thanis whispered. 'Do as I say. Don't question anything. Do you understand?'

I nodded. I had so many questions I couldn't even begin to ask them.

I wondered where the others were. I couldn't see anyone. Thanis walked straight to the centre of the circle and I followed her. The moonlight seemed stronger here. I felt like an insect trapped in amber. Time was suspended. I knew only Thanis had the power to send it spinning on its way again.

Thanis raised her hands to the sky. She began to speak in a language I'd never heard before. From somewhere in the shadow of the stones there was an answering refrain. One by one, the others joined in until their voices swept around us. Then gradually, they faded away until an intense silence reigned. It seemed an age before Thanis began to speak again, in English this time.

'O Great One, You rise from the dust. You set in the dust. Hear me now, O Golden One. You who hold eternity in your hand. Come to us. Give us your power.'

I felt as if I was in a trance when Thanis turned to me and took the rune from my neck. She held it up to the moon and continued, 'Shine your light upon us. Take back the darkness, O Mysterious One. Let your power flow through us. Let us rise from the dust of the past.'

Unexpectedly, she threw the rune to the ground. I saw the gold reflecting back the moonlight then suddenly it seemed to burst into flames. I could feel the scorching heat on my skin. I tried to move away but something held me fast. Thanis took the spiral from her own neck and fastened it around mine. I felt the life flowing back into my limbs.

She held my hand and led me around the flames. Once, twice, maybe six or seven times. Was it my imagination, or did the flames get higher and higher with each circuit we made?

'Repeat after me: Let me become like the imperishable stars.'

'Let me become like the imperishable stars,' I whispered.

'Let the arms of the night free me.'

'Let the arms of the night free me.'

'Let the eye of the sun watch over me.'

'Let the . . . ' As I began to repeat the words an incredible thing happened. The flames began to die down and the sun appeared over the horizon. ' . . . eye of the sun watch over me,' I finished, much louder this time.

We stood in silence while the sun slowly rose up into the sky.

I was filled with a sense of wonder.

'Now you are truly one with us,' Thanis told me.

'Yes.' I smiled at her. I felt perfectly calm. I didn't understand what had happened, but for once I didn't care. I trusted her completely now. All my doubts had gone.

'Come, it is over,' she said as she turned and started to leave the circle.

I was about to follow her when I looked down. The grass glistened in the early morning light. There was a fine layer of dew on each blade. Our feet had left no marks. No blade lay broken or twisted. Even stranger, there was no sign of the fire that had blazed so fiercely.

37

I awoke the next morning feeling full of life. I dressed quickly and, taking my sketch book and pencils, rushed out. I knew I had to draw. I was certain that I'd be able to create in a way I'd never been able to before. I wanted to make the most of it while it lasted. I walked down to the harbour and climbed up onto the cliffs. I walked along to a deserted bay where a dramatic group of rocks led out into the sea.

I decided to climb onto a ledge a few feet down where I would be out of sight of anyone venturing along the cliff path. My feet still seemed to have a power of their own. I had no fear of falling; I moved so easily and surely over the rocks. I discovered that below the ledge the cliff was not so sheer as it had looked. I could see a way down to the beach. I decided to climb all the way down and go out onto the rocks to draw.

My pencil flew over the pages as though it had a will of its own. Each line was so effortless. When I looked at the drawings I thought I could see the waves rolling over the page. The spray seemed to fly off the paper. The water seemed to swirl and eddy with an impossible force. I couldn't stop. I filled page after page. Each drawing was even better than the last.

In fact, all the days that followed took on the same pattern. I was totally absorbed in my work. I had to capture whatever I saw on paper. And I did. Whether it was the sea or the sky, the moors or the winding country lanes, everything seemed to transfer itself on to paper with the same outstanding force. Every place was open to me. Wherever my eye landed, my feet found a way to carry me there.

The reality around me was so strong that I forgot everything else. I was surprised when Mel stopped me one day and demanded, 'Jessica, why haven't you answered my messages?'

'Mel, I didn't realize you're back.'

'You mean you didn't get them? I've been to the house a few times but no one was in. I pushed a note through the letter box,' she said. She looked at me strangely. 'Are you all right? You look different somehow.'

'Maybe I am,' I told her. 'My work is going so well.'

'You're still finishing the spiral you showed me?' Mel asked.

'Oh no,' I said eagerly. 'I'm drawing. It's amazing how inspiring everything is here.'

'Is that them?' Mel asked, pointing at my bag. 'Can I see them?'

'Of course. But not yet.' I wasn't ready to share them with anyone yet.

'So when are you leaving?'

'Leaving?' I asked, surprised.

'Doesn't your college start again soon?'

'Not till September,' I said.

Mel stared at me, looking puzzled.

'It is September, Jessica. It's September 5th.'

38

I realized I didn't care about college any more. The only thing that mattered to me now was my art. The past no longer seemed real. Everything I needed was here. Thanis and her circle believed in me. They encouraged and praised me. I felt I belonged with them now.

Eva was the only one I wasn't comfortable with. She had lost all interest in art, her own and anyone else's. Her pale blue eyes would glaze over when I showed my drawings each evening. She never went up to her studio. She insisted she'd had enough and would never paint again.

I saw her a few times when I was out drawing. Once I caught her staring at me, but as soon as I looked up she turned away.

Another time I was sure she had followed me. I decided to confront her.

'What do you want, Eva? Why don't you leave me alone?'

She looked around anxiously before answering. I wondered if she was ill, she looked so pale and tired.

'What do I want?' she repeated, then laughed cynically. 'Oh, I want nothing at all. There's nothing in the whole world that holds any interest for me now.'

'Then why are you following me? Don't deny it. I know you are,' I told her crossly.

'I'm trying to warn you,' Eva whispered.

'Warn me? What about?' I said, not believing her for a moment.

'You've seen the paintings,' she said, 'the ones in my studio.'

'Yes.'

'When I painted them I was like you. I put my whole life into them. I couldn't bear to sell them. Now I can't bear to look at them,' she finished sadly.

'You'll paint again,' I told her. 'Everyone has bad spells. It'll come back.'

'No, you don't understand. I don't want to paint any more. I'm finished. I'm too tired.' She paused. I thought she seemed lost in her own thoughts but suddenly she grabbed my arm and said, 'You could still get away. It's not too late. Think of your friends, London. You're so young.'

I pulled my arm free. 'Don't worry about me. I can take care of myself.'

'Of course. You've chosen. Forget I said anything. I was trying to help you,' she said as she began to walk away. I noticed how slowly she moved. She didn't seem very steady on her feet. Was she ill? On impulse I ran after her.

'Are you all right?'

'That doesn't matter now. You won't tell her? Promise me that,' she said urgently.

I looked at her puzzled. 'Tell who? You mean Thanis?'

'Of course I mean Thanis,' she snapped. 'Can't you understand anything? She's dangerous. You can't trust her.'

As soon as she mentioned Thanis my sympathy withered. What was it between them?

'Why do you stay here?' I asked. 'Why don't you just leave?'

'It's too late for me. There's nowhere left for me to go,' Eva said, sinking down onto the grass. 'My bones ache.

I'm so tired.' Her eyes had a faraway look. I wasn't sure if she was talking to me or to herself.

'You need a doctor. You're ill. Why don't I go and get help?' I offered.

'No. You mustn't tell anyone.' She became agitated again and grabbed me by the shoulders. 'Promise,' she hissed.

'All right, I promise,' I said trying to pacify her.

'You won't tell anyone we met. No one. That's the safest.'

I collected my things and climbed down onto the beach. When I looked back she was still sitting there, her head resting on her knees. That was when I noticed it. Something was sitting on the rocks a few yards away from her. It looked like a large black cat.

39

I soon forgot all about Eva. When I got back to the house Thanis and Peter were waiting for me. Thanis was smiling like the proverbial cat who got the cream. She handed me a large envelope and said smiling, 'Go on, open it.'

'What is it?' I asked.

'Open it and find out for yourself,' Thanis ordered.

I tore into the envelope. Inside was a cheque for £1000. I had to stare at it for a minute or two. It definitely had my name on it.

'What's this? Is it really for me?' I kept counting the noughts. 'Who's it from?'

'It's for you,' Peter told me. 'I sold a couple of your drawings when I was in London yesterday.'

I was so surprised I didn't know what to say. I stood

staring at him. Then I rushed over and threw my arms around him. 'Thank you. You're wonderful. I want to know everything. Where did you sell them? What did they say? Did they really like them that much?'

Peter detached himself from me and said calmly, 'I sold them to a gallery that specializes in young artists. It's a good contact. You should get more for the next lot.'

'You mean they want more?' I shouted, totally over the moon by now. 'They really like me?'

'Of course they do. They had a buyer in mind when they bought them. They know their business,' Peter said, 'and so do I. There's nothing for you to worry about.'

'So, are you pleased?' Thanis asked. 'Are you happy you met me? I promised you success, and now you have it.'

'Of course I'm happy. I'm thrilled. And it's all such a surprise. I'd no idea. A thousand pounds. That's fantastic. I'm rich. Shall we celebrate? Let's go out somewhere.'

'Not tonight,' Thanis said. 'We have a big day tomorrow.'

'What's happening tomorrow?' I asked.

'I have something to show you, Jessica. It is time you began to understand.'

'Good,' I said doubtfully. I was perfectly content as I was. I didn't want anything to get in the way of my art. 'Will it take long?'

'Do not worry about time. You will have plenty of that. But there are things you must learn. I must teach you.' She gave one of her rare smiles.

It was hard for me to get to sleep that night. So many thoughts were rushing around in my head. I felt everything I'd ever dreamed of was within my reach. When, eventually, I did get to sleep my dreams were full of paintings. They were dark, stormy landscapes bathed in moonlight. They were hung in a gallery that seemed to stretch away endlessly, where the only light was from tall candles that stood at intervals on the floor. Their light was reflected dimly in the polished marble of the floor. When I looked down I saw a face staring back at me. Only it wasn't mine. It was Eva's.

40

The next morning Thanis woke me at dawn. I climbed into the car, still half asleep. She drove quickly, speeding through the twilight lanes where night still seemed to linger. There was an awful chill in the air. I realized summer was over.

'How long will we stay here?' I asked.

Thanis shrugged. She turned her head and stared at me without lowering the speed. The wheel seemed to turn of its own volition, so the car flowed effortlessly around each twist and bend. 'Not much longer. Are you ready to leave?' she said.

'Soon,' I told her.

'Soon,' she repeated. 'Yes, soon we will move on. We will be finished here.'

'What will be finished?' I asked. 'What are you waiting for?'

'For one final ceremony. We must open the way for the future,' Thanis told me.

'With the spiral?' I said enthusiastically, feeling that at last I was beginning to understand.

'Yes, of course with the spiral. The spiral is the key. That is why it is so important to us. But only after the ceremony will the gates of past and future open and allow us to pass through.'

'Oh,' I said, realizing she had lost me again.

'Nothing is certain,' Thanis said calmly, 'least of all, time.'

I wasn't any the wiser, but I realized there was no point in asking more questions. I decided to change the subject.

'What will happen afterwards? Where will you go? Will you go home?' I asked.

I saw her lips curl slightly into a smile. 'No, not home,' Thanis said. 'That is not possible. But we will be free to go where we wish. What about you? What will you do, Jessica?'

'Me? I've no idea. Perhaps I'll travel. I haven't thought about it.' That was true. I hadn't made any plans. I'd been living totally in the present. Neither past nor future seemed real.

'You can go anywhere, do anything you want,' Thanis told me.

'As long as I can paint,' I added.

'Yes,' Thanis agreed. 'You must paint. You made that choice.'

We both fell silent. Thanis had turned off the road and we were driving across a rough track. I suddenly realized we were near Nuskhet's house. I could see the headland reaching out into the sea. The water was becoming increasingly blue as the sun rose higher in the sky.

'Is this where we're going?' I asked, puzzled. I wondered why all the secrecy.

Thanis merely nodded. She seemed preoccupied. Instead of driving towards the house she pulled off the track and manoeuvred the car into the shelter of some rocks. Without answering my question she flung open the door and sprang out onto the turf.

'Follow me,' she ordered as she hurried away.

'Where are we going?' I asked. I had to run to catch up with her. She ignored my question and kept walking.

When she reached the cliff edge she stood for a moment

looking out at the sea. As I came up behind her I saw her silhouetted against the sky. She seemed balanced on the edge of infinity. I thought she might just step over the edge and expect me to follow her. I thought maybe I would too.

'At last,' Thanis said impatiently. 'The tide is just right for us. Follow carefully. This way.'

She eased herself over the cliff edge and jumped down to a group of rocks that jutted out from the cliff face. Below her was a drop of eighty feet but she moved as fearlessly as a cat, landing effortlessly. She signalled to me to follow and I had no choice but to jump too. There was no other way down. I landed on my knees and had to cling to the rocks until I regained my balance. I could hear the pebbles on the beach being washed back and forth in the pull of the tide, just as they had from the beginning of time.

I looked around. I couldn't see how we were going to get anywhere from here. As I opened my mouth to speak Thanis raised a hand to silence me.

'Watch and follow,' she commanded. I watched in amazement as Thanis slid into a narrow gap between two rocks and seemed to disappear into the cliff face. 'Come,' I heard her voice call back to me. I stared in disbelief at the rocks. How could anyone get through here? I was certain I couldn't.

'There is no time to waste. Just follow. Do not question,' Thanis ordered as if she had read my mind. I sighed angrily, but moved my hand obediently over the cold surface of the rock. To my surprise it slipped easily through the narrow gap. I eased my arm and leg in after it then held my breath and squeezed through into the darkness. When I looked back I could just see a tiny strip of sky.

It took my eyes a while to adjust to the darkness. I realized we were in one of the tunnels that networked through the cliffs under Nuskhet's house. Thanis had not waited but had gone on ahead. I couldn't hear her footsteps but she had left behind a faint whiff of her scent. The floor of the tunnel sloped steeply downwards. I could hear water trickling somewhere near and, much further away, the sound of waves. Where was she leading me? The sky seemed such a long way away. I longed to breathe fresh air.

'Thanis,' I whispered softly. 'Thanis, where are you?' My voice died away leaving the silence more intense than ever. When I looked behind me there was no sign of daylight. I had no choice but to go on. The deeper I went the louder the sound of the waves became. Then suddenly, I reached a dead end. I was sure I'd taken a wrong turning.

Then I saw it, at the end of the tunnel there was a narrow gap between the rocks. When I knelt down I could hear the sea surging angrily below. A bitterly cold breeze carrying faint splashes of spray reached my face. 'Thanis?' I whispered again. Still there was no reply. I lowered my feet through the gap and felt them swing hopelessly in the damp air. Praying I wasn't making a big mistake, I squeezed myself through and hung for a moment suspended in the void. When I managed to open my eyes I thought I'd had it. Below me the water rushed frantically around a vast cave, crashing against the seaweed covered walls and sending spray flying everywhere.

I could just make out a narrow ledge of rock to my right. I freed my left hand and forced myself to swing across to it. As far as I could tell it looked secure. I let myself drop down. My feet scrambled over the damp, slippy surface. I felt myself sliding towards the waiting sea. The waves reached up and broke around my ankles. I could feel them trying to drag me down. My fingers scrabbled over the rock but it had been polished smooth by untold centuries of waves. There was nothing for me to cling to.

I hadn't time to be afraid. Suddenly the water was all around me. I was dragged down into a swirling mass. I could hear my heart beating wildly. There was salt water in my mouth, in my lungs. Why wasn't I dead? I felt as if I'd been trapped in the swirling waves for ever. I opened my eyes. Why didn't the salt sting? I could just see through the murky waters. There was something shining in the distance. I made a huge effort and threw myself towards it.

41

As if through a curtain of water, I saw Thanis standing with a burning torch. Around her the shadows seemed to dance. The waves rose up yet fell away from her. Her eyes were full of darkness. Her hair shone in the firelight. I knew then she wasn't human. But it was too late. I had to trust her. There was no other escape.

'At last. Hurry up,' she said, turning away.

I found my feet were touching solid ground. I rose awkwardly to my knees and dragged myself up onto higher ground.

'I'm not wet,' I said in amazement. 'What happened?'

'You passed through a doorway. That is all,' she replied enigmatically.

'But the sea?' I looked back at the swirling mass of dark water. 'I don't understand.'

'Of course you don't. Not now. But with time, then, yes, I think you will. The elements are not our enemies, Jessica. We are as fire and wind and wave. They cannot destroy us. You must not fear them. You must learn to respect them before you can truly share their power.'

'Why did you bring me here?' I asked.

'There is something you must see. We are almost there. Now we must hurry or we will be trapped by the tide.' She led me through a tunnel that descended even deeper into the earth. The air was dank and heavy with the smell of the seaweed that grew everywhere. I realized the tunnel would flood as the tide rose. No wonder Thanis was in such a hurry.

I was relieved when Thanis stopped. The tunnel had opened into a slightly wider space. Thanis held the torch so I could see the bare rock above the high water mark. As I looked up I saw something glimmering in the firelight.

'Look around you. What do you see?' she said.

'It's . . . it's silver,' I whispered. 'You got it here, didn't you? The silver for the spiral.'

'Yes. I wanted you to see this. Once there was much silver here,' Thanis said sadly. 'Now, this is the last. You must use it wisely.'

'That's why the house is here, isn't it?' I asked.

'Yes. Nuskhet has guarded this place for a long time. Now, no more questions.'

She lowered the torch and strode off into the darkness. I hurried after her, determined not to be left behind again. As I walked the cave came alive around me as the light caught the faint silver seams in the rock.

'Is this the way out?' I asked hopefully.

Thanis didn't bother to answer. I had no idea what was going to happen. I was only too aware of all the darkness gathered around us. Of the waves getting louder. Of the sea creeping slowly in. Of the sky so far away.

At last she stopped. 'This is where the power is strongest. What do you see?' Thanis said.

I looked around, puzzled. 'Nothing,' I said. 'It's too dark.'

'There is no time to waste,' she said angrily. 'Have you learned nothing! Use your senses. Look.'

'What's that?' I asked. I was sure I'd heard something.

'Only the sea,' Thanis replied.

I looked around but I couldn't see anything in the dark.

'It sounds more like an animal,' I said. I'd started to shiver. The air seemed colder and damper than ever. I had a vision of

107

the tide creeping in through those long, dark tunnels. I longed to be back where there was sunshine and fresh air.

'Yes, you are right,' Thanis said. 'It is time to leave. You must hurry. Concentrate. Clear your mind.'

I was sure the breeze was getting stronger. Somehow I knew the tide was getting closer. The first of the waves would soon be breaking around our feet. This was madness. I had to get out.

'No.' Thanis grabbed my arm. 'Give up now and I will leave you here. You must look. Tell me what you see. There is no other way out.'

I had no choice. I knew she would carry out her threat. I looked around once more. All I could see were the shadows cast by the torch flickering on the walls. Nothing relieved the darkness. There was no silver here. No hidden seams of metal in the rock. I knelt down, feeling the surface of the cold rock with my fingers. Why was there no seaweed here? My fingers moved more quickly. Was there something?

'Here. Give me the torch,' I shouted.

I jammed the torch into a crevice and refocused my eyes as the flames cast their light onto the floor by my feet. The smoke made my eyes water but I had to persevere. I thought I'd seen something. 'Is this it? Help me,' I shouted.

'No one can help you. You must do it. Hurry.'

My fingers worked quickly. There was some irregularity in the surface here. I traced it round and round. It seemed to be a . . . a spiral. I could hardly believe it. I looked up in amazement. Thanis was laughing at me.

'At last,' she said. 'I thought you would never find it. You are so slow sometimes.'

'Is it a spiral?' I asked quietly. 'How did it get here?'

'Who knows. Ask the ocean if it made it. Ask the darkness what it saw. Why ask me? It has been there for millennia, long before my time.'

'But you knew it was there. You wanted me to find it. I don't understand. Why is it so important?' I felt tired and confused. Angry. Disappointed. I'd risked my life for this. And I still didn't understand anything.

'Come. There is no time to waste. No, not that way. This is the way out. Give me the torch.'

At the back of the cave there was a pile of loose boulders which Thanis climbed nimbly. I followed behind her, struggling to keep my balance. At the top was another opening that led into a narrow passageway which we had to crawl through. I could feel the weight of the granite pressing against my back. Drops of icy cold water trickled through my jumper. I think we crawled for about a hundred metres before we joined another tunnel. I was relieved to be able to stand up. The air was much better here too.

Thanis seemed to know the place well. We passed other tunnels leading away in all directions. The place was a veritable labyrinth. I would never have found my way out alone. At last I felt a blast of fresh air fill my lungs and knew the surface was near. We turned a sharp corner and the sudden sunlight stung my eyes. We came out on top of a tumulus between the flat stones of an ancient tor. I could see the sea far away in the distance. Nuskhet's house was just visible. We must have been underground for hours because the sun was directly overhead.

'You have survived. I had my doubts,' Thanis said. 'You have passed through fire, water, earth, and air. Now you will be strong. But you still have much to learn. Promise me you will never go below alone. It is too dangerous for you. The sea comes in so quickly. If you are trapped, escape is impossible.'

'I won't,' I said. 'Definitely not. I can promise you that. It's so strange down there. The sea sounded like some kind of animal. It was spooky.'

'It is another world below. You would do well to remember that, Jessica.'

As we started the long walk back to the car I was sure nothing would ever get me in that maze of tunnels again.

42

We drove back to the house in silence. I needed to be alone with my thoughts. I asked Thanis to drop me off at the next village so I could walk back along the cliff path. As I watched the car speed away I wondered if I'd ever understand Thanis. I suspected that not everything she demanded of me was really necessary. She seemed addicted to drama and had to make a mystery out of everything. Then again, I wasn't sure. Had my life really been in danger this morning?

I climbed up the steep path from the village and soon found my mood lifting. I'd become so much stronger since I'd been here I could walk long distances effortlessly. Now the summer season was over the crowds had gone, although I still overtook a few walkers as I hurried along the narrow path. I'd grown to love the wildness almost as much as Thanis. I didn't want the view spoilt by people. I wanted to be alone with the sky and the sea.

I'd been walking for a couple of hours when I spotted a figure sitting on some rocks in the distance. As I drew nearer the figure began to seem familiar. I was unlikely to come across anyone else with that particularly bright shade of red on their hair. I wasn't surprised when a voice shouted, 'Jessica,' and the figure began to wave enthusiastically at me.

'Mel, what a surprise,' I said bleakly.

'I've been waiting for you,' she said.

'For me?'

'Yes, Thanis told me you'd be coming this way.'

'Did she?' I was puzzled. I knew she didn't like Mel.

'She seems to be in a good mood today.' Mel smiled. 'She's not usually so friendly when I knock at your door. What have you two been up to? Been out on your broomsticks?'

I forced myself to smile at her joke. I didn't want company, but now Mel was here I'd have to spend some time with her. I tried to think of something to say, but before I could she'd continued, 'How've you been? I haven't seen you for ages. I thought maybe you'd gone back to London. Aren't you going back to college?'

'I've been busy,' I said. I thought how out of place Mel seemed here on the clifftop. She was wearing a purple jacket that clashed with her hair and a pair of khaki trousers. 'Working. You know what it's like.'

'My season's over. I'm just waiting for Jack, then we'll be off somewhere hot for a few weeks. Maybe India. So when are you leaving?'

I shrugged. I couldn't remember why I'd ever liked Mel. As the words spilled out of her in an endless stream I longed for silence. Her voice was really irritating me.

'Jessica? Are you all right? There isn't anything wrong, is there?' She was giving me a puzzled look.

'No, I'm fine,' I said. I paused.

'You're not going back to college, are you?'

'No, I'm not. I've sold some of my work.'

'That's great. But are you sure you won't regret it later? And what about Jim?' Mel looked concerned. 'You haven't had another row or anything?'

For a moment I couldn't understand what she was talking about. I was still trying to find a noncommittal answer when she went on, 'Jessica, are you sure you're OK? You seem different somehow. His name was Jim, wasn't it? Or have I got muddled up?'

'Jim? Oh yes, I'd for—' I stopped myself just in time. 'I expect he's OK. He's probably at college again now.'

'You don't seem sure,' Mel said. 'Haven't you spoken to

him?' She was looking at me oddly. I wished she'd mind her own business.

'Like I said, I've been busy.'

'Have you had a row? I thought you were really missing him. Have you met someone else, is that it?'

'No, it's just what I said. I've been busy. My work's all that matters to me now. That's going really well.'

'That's what you said last time I saw you,' Mel reminded me. 'I'd love to see your work. You said you'd been out drawing?'

'Yes.'

'What? Landscape?' She waited a few seconds for an answer before repeating, 'Landscapes, is that what you're drawing?'

I turned to look at her. It was hard to drag my eyes away from the waves breaking far out in the ocean. I was aware that the wind was gaining force all the time. 'Sorry, I was . . . You were asking about my drawings. Yes, I suppose they are landscapes.'

'Can I see them?' Mel was persistent.

'I don't have much with me,' I said. 'Just a couple of sketches in my pocket book.' I handed it over to her without enthusiasm.

Mel took the book and stood looking through it slowly. I turned back to the ocean and my own thoughts. I didn't care about her opinion. It seemed strange that I ever had. Mel was unusually silent for a few minutes.

'Wow, you have changed,' she said when she'd finally finished. 'This is powerful stuff. It's not like you at all. I mean, I didn't mean . . . I just mean it's not what I was expecting.' She looked worried.

'That's OK,' I said coldly. 'I have changed. I'm a real artist now.' I thought about the big cheque I had stored away in my room.

'Of course you are. Don't be offended. Me and my big mouth. I didn't mean anything.' Mel shivered and hugged herself. 'It's getting cold. Shall we start back? I think I sat here too long. I'm freezing.'

'Go on,' I said. 'I think I'll stay here a bit longer. I'll see you later.'

'Come with me, Jessica, or I'll think I have offended you. Come back and have tea with me,' Mel pleaded.

I'd really had enough of Mel that day. I don't know why I thought what I did. The picture just came into my head. I wanted to be alone. I couldn't stop myself wishing it. Somehow the two things got confused. My wish. The picture of Mel missing her footing. I didn't do anything. The two things just connected themselves. I wasn't guilty. It was only a coincidence that I wished I was alone at exactly the same time as Mel started to slip over the edge of the cliff. Just a coincidence.

43

Even today, that image is as clear as ever. No detail has faded. Nothing has become confused or dimmed by time. There was the sudden wind that seemed to come from nowhere. There were the white crests of the waves that broke as far as the eye could see. And there was Mel's white face suspended in space, her hair a startling red against the pure blue of the sky.

There was a moment of absolute stillness, as if we had both stepped outside time. We stared at each other, shocked, uncomprehending. Then reality struck. Gravity took hold and Mel let out a weak, hoarse scream as she started to slide down the cliff face. I watched helplessly as her hand reached out towards mine. A hand that became smaller and smaller as she was carried inexorably down to the waiting rocks.

Did I really hear the sound of bones breaking when she finally hit the ground? They tell me that's impossible, that the distance was too great. They said it must have been my imagination. I'm not convinced. I remember there was another scream, much louder and stronger than before. But they tell me that was me. The people who found me said they heard it a mile away. They said I screamed and screamed endlessly, but I don't remember that. Just as I don't remember waiting for the rescue service, or talking to the police, or how Thanis got there.

Thanis dealt with most of the questions. She told the police who Mel was and where she lived. She described how she'd dropped me off and how I could have had no idea I would meet Mel that afternoon. She insisted I was too shocked to answer questions and led me home, still wrapped in the grey blanket that one of the medics had given me.

44

The inquest was held in Penzance a few days later. I'd recovered enough by then to give my evidence calmly. As I said, I remember everything that led up to Mel's fall clearly. The coroner announced a verdict of accidental death. He said it was a warning not to go too near the cliff edge. Went on about a young life wasted. Mel's husband Jack sat stiff and pale in the front row.

Afterwards Peter and Thanis took me for lunch in one of the narrow streets that led off the waterfront. Eva was supposed to join us, but she hadn't been well and rang to say she wouldn't make it. Everyone seemed subdued that day. I ordered fish but struggled to eat it. Thanis was unusually quiet. Peter seemed preoccupied. I thought perhaps he was worried about Eva. We didn't stay in the restaurant long. Thanis said she wanted to stay and do some shopping so Peter and I took the bus home.

I couldn't stay indoors. I needed to be out under the sky. I'd avoided the sea since the accident, so I took my sketchbook and some coloured pens and went to sit in the garden. There were still a few late roses in flower, but when I got close I could see their petals were already beginning to shrivel and brown at the edges. The fruit was just ripening on the ancient apple trees. It was sunny, but even in the shelter of the wall there was a chill in the air.

I started to draw and didn't look up from my work until an unexpected shadow fell across my paper. It was Eva.

'I warned you,' she whispered.

'What?' I said, crossly.

'You heard me. Don't pretend you don't know what I'm talking about,' Eva replied. She lowered herself awkwardly onto the grass next to me.

'Why don't you leave me alone? I don't need this right now,' I told her.

'Oh no? I think you do. You need help.' Eva adjusted her position carefully as if she was in pain. I noticed the skin on her calves was dry and flaking. She fingered the fabric of her skirt nervously as she spoke.

'I'm not a child. I know what I'm doing,' I said. For some reason the picture of Mel flashed through my mind. I pushed it away immediately. I picked up my pencil again and began to draw Eva half-heartedly.

We sat in silence for a few minutes. I couldn't interpret the expression in her pale blue eyes. She seemed so far away

I thought she'd forgotten I was there until she bent forward and whispered, 'Go home, Jessica. Go now, today.'

I ignored her and carried on sketching. I kept my eyes on the paper, aware she was trying to get me to look at her.

'I warned you there would be a price to pay,' she said sadly, 'but you wouldn't listen. You must listen to me now. It might be your last chance.'

'OK,' I said. 'Just what is it that you're so worried about?'

'I think you've discovered that for yourself. You've felt the power. You've already seen what terrible consequences it can have.' Eva picked up my pencil and drew a quick sketch in my book. When I looked down Mel's face stared back at me. My eyes filled with tears.

'It was an accident,' I whispered hoarsely.

'You can't believe that,' she said softly. 'It's not too late for you. At least, I hope not. You're talented. You could succeed on your own. You don't need them.'

For a moment I was tempted to believe she meant well. I felt a sudden longing for London and the life I'd left behind. I wanted to forget all of them. To forget everything that had happened. To go back to being a student, to being ordinary. For a brief moment it even seemed possible. Then I remembered Mel.

'It's too late,' I said. 'I can't go back now. Anyhow, you stayed. Why should I be any different?'

'Because everything's easier for women now,' she said crossly, perhaps sensing defeat. 'In my day I had no choice. Women weren't taken seriously as artists. I had no freedom. I wasn't allowed out of the house on my own. You can't begin to imagine what it was like then. I had no money, no way to support myself. When Thanis came it seemed like the answer to all my prayers.'

'How did you meet her?' I asked.

'In Switzerland, a long, long time ago.' Her voice softened and a dreamy expression crossed her face. 'I remember it was very early in the morning. I'd gone out to paint before everyone else was awake. It was the only time I got to myself, you see. I loved to watch the sun rise over the mountains.'

'So what happened?'

'That morning I was so absorbed in my painting—I couldn't get the colours right—that I didn't know anyone was there. Then this voice came out of the blue. ''Try adding a shadow there,'' it said. I could see immediately it would work. It did. The whole painting came to life somehow.'

I could imagine the scene clearly. 'Yes,' I said. 'That's how it was with me too.' For the first time I felt sympathetic towards her. 'But what went wrong?'

'Nothing, at first. I'd never been happier. I learned to work with gold. Thanis wanted the rune, you see. She needed it, they all did. Just as they need the spiral now. I didn't even think about it. I had no suspicions.'

Eva fell silent for a few moments, then continued, 'When I first met Thanis she was everything I'd dreamed a woman could be. She had the freedom I craved. She fascinated me. She talked as no one I'd ever heard before. She convinced me the time would come when women would be free, when women would do all the things that men had always done. Of course, I wanted to see that time for myself. I wanted the freedom she offered. Then, when I met Peter it all seemed so easy, so right. I couldn't wait to join them.'

Her face grew sad. She smoothed her skirt around her ankles, then hugged her knees. Her head began to droop and I thought she was about to fall asleep.

'Eva,' I said gently, 'are you all right?'

'No, but that doesn't matter now. My time is past. I don't belong here any more.'

'Of course you do,' I tried to assure her. 'You're ill, that's all. You need help. You're still young,' I told her.

'Oh, I'm young, am I?' Eva sneered. She started to laugh to herself. 'You don't know what you're talking about. No,

117

forgive me. I didn't come here to fight with you.' She sighed and turned her head away.

'This is your house, isn't it?' I asked. Eva nodded. 'Then why not just ask us to leave?'

'It wouldn't do any good. There's no way out for me. I need them now. But you're different. You're talented. You can succeed without them. The barriers to women have gone,' Eva said. The late afternoon sunlight showed how exhausted she looked.

'You talk as though you've come from the dark ages,' I joked.

Eva turned her pale eyes towards me and just stared for a moment or two. Then she shook her head.

'I've tried, you'll remember that, won't you?' she asked.

I felt something stirring at the back of my mind, as if some of the pieces of the puzzle were about to fall into place. 'Eva,' I began, 'how old are you?'

I saw a faint gleam in her eye. 'Maybe there is hope for you yet,' she said smiling. 'I'm . . . aahh.' She'd suddenly doubled over in pain. All the colour had rushed from her face.

'Eva, what's wrong?' I asked anxiously. 'Eva?'

'Beware of the cats,' she whispered, slowly straightening herself.

I looked around. 'I can't see a cat anywhere,' I said, puzzled.

She shook her head but couldn't speak. When I followed the direction of her eyes, I saw Thanis framed in the living room window. I was sure she was watching us.

45

Eva tried to get on to her feet, but the effort was too much for her.

'Stay here, I'll get help,' I told her.

She nodded unprotestingly, hiding her face between her hands. There were faint brown patches on her skin which I'd never noticed before. As I got up from the grass Peter came running down the gravel path.

'Eva, what happened?' he shouted. 'Here, help me.' I held her arm while Peter pulled her to her feet. She stood for a moment, swaying slightly, then her whole body slowly started to crumple. Peter caught her as she fell and lifted her up into his arms.

'Thanis is getting the car out,' he shouted to me. 'Pack a few things for her, will you?'

'Of course,' I told him. I ran into the house and hurried upstairs to their room. When I pushed open the door I was struck by how airless it was. I could see dust motes sparkling in the late afternoon sun and there was an awful sickroom smell. I wanted to open all the windows and let the fresh air flow through everything.

As I hurried towards the desk I had to avoid all the heavy furniture that was crammed into the room. Some of it was even older than I'd remembered. It belonged in a museum. At least there someone would look after it, not leave it to rot slowly away as it was here.

I grabbed some clothes, then threw some of her cosmetics, a towel, and dressing gown into a bag I found in the wardrobe and hurried downstairs after Peter. He was just putting Eva down gently on the back seat of the car when I got there. Thanis was already in the seat, tapping her fingers impatiently on the steering wheel.

'Shall I come with you?' I asked as I handed her the bag.

'No, stay here,' Thanis ordered. 'We'll come back for you later.'

I tried to get a glimpse of Eva, but she was curled up on the back seat, her pale hair falling over her face. I was relieved when I saw her shudder. At least she was still alive.

Peter climbed into the front seat, slamming the door behind him. Thanis already had the engine running and the car leapt forward and sped away up the lane. I stood and watched it go. For the first time, I felt really alone. Everything had turned sour. I felt a strange resistance to going back into that empty house, but there was nowhere else to go.

46

I don't know how I survived that night. As darkness fell I became increasingly anxious. I wished I knew where the others had gone. I felt sure Eva had been about to tell me something just before she collapsed. Now I didn't know what to believe, or who to trust. I couldn't make sense of anything and I couldn't get rid of the nagging doubts that kept turning round and round in my brain.

Why did Eva's story sound so like mine? What was she trying to warn me about? I went over everything that had happened again and again, but I couldn't find any answers to my questions. It was like a puzzle with missing pieces. I had the horrible feeling that I had all the pieces somewhere, if only I could remember where I'd put them. My mind kept turning back to that very first day in the museum. Was there some clue there that I'd missed?

I looked at my watch. It was almost nine. They'd been gone for about three hours. I wished they'd come back. It was getting dark. I felt so isolated. What if I was in danger? That thought made me even more nervous. I turned on all the lights and closed the curtains but still couldn't relax. Each time the wind rattled the windows or a floorboard creaked on the stairs I jumped. I kept imagining footsteps on the gravel outside. I froze when I heard a door bang upstairs.

I was too wound up to go to bed so I started to draw. It was soothing to watch the pencil move back and forth across the paper. It was satisfying to make the shadows darker and darker. I put the sketchbook down and made myself a cup of coffee. When I came back I was surprised by what I'd drawn. That shadow I'd worked so hard on looked just like a cat. I felt its eyes staring at me from the depths of the paper. No, I was getting too jumpy. I closed the book and threw it away. A few minutes later I went to look at it again. It was just a sketch. There wasn't a cat in it anywhere.

I told myself I must have heard a cat out in the garden. There were always cats out there, especially at night. I remembered Mel's birds and shivered. Why didn't someone come home and tell me what was happening? I felt abandoned. What if they never came back? No, that was crazy. I had to calm down. I should go to bed. Was that a car parking? I went to the window but couldn't see anything past the old, ivy covered wall. I waited and listened. Was that the gate creaking? Surely that was a footstep.

It must have been around midnight when the cats began to howl. Then there was the sound of claws scraping on glass. Something started to wail pathetically. If I stared out of the window long enough I could see things moving in the shadows everywhere. I had to go to bed. Try to sleep. I was driving myself crazy like this.

I forced myself out into the dimly lit passage and up the stairs. I left all the lights on downstairs. Now, hurrying along the corridor to my room, the dark doorways of the empty rooms confronted me. My imagination was working overtime. I knew I'd never sleep unless I reassured myself everything was OK.

I turned the light on in Thanis's room. Of course there was nothing there. I noticed the cupboard door where she kept the mummified cat was slightly ajar. I stopped myself going over and closing it. I wasn't going to let myself be scared of a dead cat. I crossed the room and closed the curtains. By the window there was a small table with a collection of antiquities laid out haphazardly on its surface. There was a blue glazed scarab, about two inches long, a tiny clay cat, a few amulets carved from semi-precious stones and a fragment of wood roughly painted with the figure of a winged sphinx. I felt something stir in the depths of my mind, as if a memory was about to surface. But I lost it.

I switched off the light, closed the door, and crossed the corridor to Eva's room. I'd left it in more of a mess than I'd realized when I was searching for things she might need in hospital. I went in and started to tidy the clothes falling out of the wardrobe. It was an enormous piece of furniture, about eight feet wide, divided into three sections, with a full length mirror attached to the back of one of the doors. I picked up a silk dress and put it back on a hanger.

The wardrobe was so packed I had to force everything back to fit it in. I couldn't resist flicking through the rail of clothes. The smart tailored suits and dresses I recognized were all hanging in the central section, but pushed back to each side I found a strange assortment of period clothes. There were delicate twenties dresses handsewn with tiny glass beads, fifties ballgowns, their voluminous skirts squashed and creased, heavy taffeta creations that must have been Victorian. As I took them out there was a smell of mothballs, dust, and stale perfume.

On a shelf in the top was an assortment of old boxes. Here I found the shoes and bags, each carefully wrapped in tissue paper so old that it disintegrated at my touch. Some of them belonged in a museum. I was so absorbed by what I'd found that I forgot all about my nerves. An idea was stirring at the back of my mind, but it was so preposterous that I couldn't accept it.

I was so preoccupied as I closed the wardrobe doors that at first I thought nothing of the figure I saw reflected in the mirror.

Then it slowly dawned on me. I wasn't alone. I spun around quickly but the room was empty.

'Thanis?' I said quietly. I was sure I'd seen her. At least I thought it was her, although the face had been in shadow. I tiptoed across the room and stood by the door listening. The house was in total silence. It was too quiet. The wind had dropped and even the cats had stopped wailing.

I dropped down onto the bed and curled up. I closed my eyes as tightly as I could. I thought about Eva. If it was her spirit I'd seen it could only mean one thing.

47

I didn't sleep much that night. I lay on Eva's bed praying for daylight. Praying for the sun to rise and chase away all the crazy ideas that had taken root in my head. I was so tense I ached everywhere. I couldn't bear it if Eva was dead too. I hadn't trusted her and now it was too late.

I must have fallen asleep eventually because the next thing I knew someone was shaking my shoulder. I opened my eyes slowly and looked up in a daze. Thanis was bending over me. She looked as calm as ever. For a moment I couldn't remember where I was. Then, slowly, everything came back to me.

'Eva?' I whispered. 'Is she . . . '

'She should be OK,' Thanis said.

'Then she's not dead?' I felt relief flood over me.

'Dead? Why should she be dead? Really, Jessica, I'm surprised at you. What are you doing in here, by the way?' Thanis sat down on the edge of the bed and examined her long fingernails.

I didn't answer immediately. I arranged the pillows against the headboard and leaned back against them. 'Tell me everything,' I said.

Thanis raised her eyebrows slightly and smiled. 'Everything?' She rubbed her hands over her forehead and pushed the heavy hair back off her face. 'Are you sure? Think carefully.'

'Yes. You know what I mean. I want to know the truth. You've been keeping things from me.' I forced myself to keep looking at her. I wanted an answer.

'That is not so easy. Exactly what do you feel you need to know?'

'Well, about Eva for a start. How old is she?' I said calmly.

'Ah, so you have realized that. A few hundred years, I forget exactly,' Thanis said.

I gasped. I hadn't expected that.

'I thought you had guessed.'

'Then you . . . ' I stared at Thanis. She shrugged.

'Now you understand why I could not tell you. You would not have believed me. It was not necessary for you to know.'

'I think I would have noticed eventually.' I paused while the information sunk in. It was hard for my brain to accept it. I stared at Thanis. She looked so normal, so healthy. The sunlight was streaming in through the window. Her skin, her hair, her elegance and style. How could there be anything supernatural about her?

'No, you are not dreaming. You always asked too many questions, Jessica. Now you must deal with the answers. I told you my culture was very old.'

'What are you?' I asked. I had to force my voice to speak. 'What do you want with me?'

'More questions?' She sneered, tossing her hair. 'Is that because you are afraid of the answers? Your world is so ignorant. Ignorant.' She spat the words out. 'You are so proud of your knowledge, your science. Puh, it is nothing. Nothing.' She leaned forward and glared at me angrily. I forced myself to meet her gaze. I had to know. I couldn't give up now. 'My culture was thousands of years old when you were still living like animals. We had everything, did you know that? We understood the earth and the heavens. We had such cities, such art, science you cannot dream of. The gods walked with us, shared their secrets, their powers. Now this, this world of yours. You can't imagine how I despise it.'

'Then why me? What do you want with me?' I asked.

'You still don't understand, do you? I needed the spiral. The symbol is the life. I told you.'

'Then you're alive because of me?' I gasped.

'Yes, because of you, Jessica. And before you, Eva. And before her someone else, and so on and so on. Now do you understand? Do you? Are you happy now you know everything? That is what you wanted, isn't it?' She flung her head back and burst into laughter.

I swung my legs to the ground and stood up cautiously. Her arm shot out and closed around mine.

'You chose,' she whispered. 'Now you must go on. Come, get your coat. There is much to do.'

48

My mind was spinning so fast as we raced across the countryside that I could barely speak. What had I done? No, it was unthinkable. It couldn't be true. I didn't want it to be true. It had to be a trick. A nasty, evil trick they were playing on me. But why? What had I done to make them hate me?

But the evidence. There were the old clothes, the photos. All that could be faked. So why wasn't I convinced? Why did I have that horrible feeling in the pit of my stomach? Why was I so sure Thanis had told me the truth?

'Where are we going?' I said.

'I am taking you to see Eva. That is what you wanted, isn't it?' Thanis said calmly. She was driving faster than ever. The small fields and hedges were reduced to almost a blur. The driving had put her in a better mood. She seemed amused by my turmoil.

'To a hospital?' I was puzzled. We were driving away from any town, towards the wild moorland.

'My poor Jessica. This really is difficult for you, isn't it? It is all much too soon. You should have trusted me. Waited. You would have learned all in time. We have so much of it.'

'We? You don't mean . . .'

'Yes, you are one with us now. I thought you understood that. It was your choice, remember. No one has forced you.'

I stared at her in horror. Her lips were curled into an ironic smile. How could she remain so calm, so unconcerned? Didn't she care about my feelings at all?

'You'll get used to it. You will even enjoy it. You are lucky. Many people would envy you.'

'I didn't know. I'd no idea. I don't want it. No,' I broke off, almost sobbing. What had I done?

49

'See, here is Eva. Alive and well,' Thanis said as she flung open the door. We were in Nuskhet's house. Eva looked up from her book and nodded to me. She looked much better than yesterday. Her skin had lost its deathly pallor and there was an air of energy about her.

'Jessica knows everything,' Thanis said, 'so you don't need to warn her any more.'

Eva turned away from her. 'I am well again, thanks to Nuskhet. I will go on living.' Her voice was emotionless. She went back to her book and ignored us.

Thanis crossed to the window and stood looking out at the sea. It was perfectly calm that day, blue and tranquil. It struck me how inappropriate that was. I felt there should be storms, thunder crashing all around us, waves lashing up the cliffs, spray flung against the window panes. And Thanis herself looked far from the monster that she was. Her hair was pinned up neatly. She wore a knee length skirt that wouldn't have been out of place in an office and a green sweater that matched the colour of her eyes.

'So, what happens now?' I said. 'Am I a prisoner?'

'Of course not. Really, Jessica. You must curb your imagination. You can go anywhere you like. We are not your enemy. You are one with us.' Thanis paused briefly. 'Actually, I wish you would go out. This is becoming tedious. Go, get some fresh air. Breathe deeply. Come back when you are in a better mood.'

'I'll go with you,' Eva said. 'If that's OK with you?'

'Of course,' I told her. 'If you're sure you're well enough.'

'She'll be fine. Don't worry about her,' Thanis said. 'Try to enjoy life. You are going to have so much of it.'

'Come on, this way,' Eva said. She showed no sign of the fatigue that she'd been suffering for the past couple of weeks. She was wearing the thin summer trousers I'd packed for her and a small tight sweater that barely reached her waist. 'We'll go where they can't see us. Then we can talk properly.'

She led me away from the sea, towards the tor where I'd emerged from the tunnel that day that seemed an age ago. 'We're not going underground, are we?'

'No, if we cut across here we will reach the next bay. Away from their influence,' Eva said. 'Look, from here you can see the ocean on both sides of the peninsula. This is the edge of the world. It is getting harder and harder to find such places. Even they will not last forever. The time will come when there are no wild places left. All the power will be gone.'

'You make that sound sad,' I said. 'I thought you hated them.'

'No, only myself. I blame myself for staying so long. I could have gone. Now it's too late.'

'Who are they, Eva? Is it really true? Are they really so old?'

'Yes, unbelievable as it is. I think they go back to ancient times. They have used their power to cheat death. They cling to life. I don't understand why. You'd think they'd be tired of it by now.'

'Are there many of them?' I asked. I wanted to know the worst.

'Not now. At least, I don't think so,' Eva said.

We'd reached the next bay and took a narrow path that zigzagged down the cliff to the beach. It was so peaceful in the autumn sun, gulls circled above us. Out in the bay a grey seal bobbed up and down near the rocky island that rose a few feet above the waves.

'So they're immortal?' I asked when we finally reached the fine, white sand.

'No, not exactly. They can die. I think you have seen this yourself.'

'I have?'

'Yes, think back. How was Thanis when you first met her?'

'She was . . . yes, I think I see what you mean. She was ill. That was how I met her. She fell, stumbled. But I'm not sure. Maybe it was an act. A trap.' That first day in the museum. I had never found out what had been wrong with her. 'There was another time too. She looked terrible. Almost like another person.'

'When the power fails them, that is what happens.'

'So then they need the symbol?' I asked.

'Yes, that is some of it. The symbol gives them their power. But they have their healers too. Bone setters they call them in their language. They've never forgotten the ancient arts.'

'Bone setters? Then I did break my ankle!' I exclaimed. I told Eva about the time I'd fallen in the cave and Nuskhet had placed his hands on my ankle.

We were silent for some minutes. Eva seemed lost in thought. Her eyes were fixed on the horizon where a lone boat lingered on the edge of the ocean. As she sat she ran her fingers through the sand.

'What will you do now?' I asked quietly.

Eva shrugged. She picked up a handful of the fine white sand and let it run between her fingers. 'I'll stay.'

'Will you be all right?'

'You mean, will I go on living? Yes, for a while. Until the next time. Maybe then I'll be brave enough to crawl away, find a place to hide and die in peace,' she said.

'I'm so afraid,' I said. 'Will I have to stay here?'

'No. Everything will happen as you wished, that is the worst. You'll have all the success you dreamed of. You'll do everything you ever wanted,' Eva said sadly. 'But in the end, yes. You will come back to them. There's nowhere else to go.'

50

'Feeling better?' Thanis said, raising an eyebrow, when we returned to the house. Eva ignored her. She picked up her book and said she was going upstairs. 'What about you, Jessica? How are you?'

'Don't pretend you care about me,' I answered crossly.

'Of course I care. We all do. In time you will understand.'

I shuddered. Time. How I hated that word. 'Eva said I'm free to leave. Is that true? I can go back to London?'

'To your little flat in Camden Town? To the dirt and noise and traffic? If that is your choice, then yes, you can.'

'Then I will,' I told her. 'I'll go now.' I got up from the chair as I spoke.

'Not now,' Thanis ordered. 'You must stay for the Ceremony.'

'And if I don't? What will happen then?'

'I will not be able to protect you,' she said, looking at me sadly. After a pause she continued, 'In any case, there is still much for you to learn. No, you must listen to me. Sit. You must learn to use the power wisely or it will use you. You have already had one accident. I think you don't want any more.'

As she spoke I could hear Mel's scream, hoarse with surprise, echoing through my mind. I slumped back down into the chair and started to untie my trainers. All thoughts of London now seemed like a hopeless dream.

'I wish I'd never met you,' I said. 'I don't want the power.'

'I don't understand you,' Thanis said. 'I thought you were the one. You knew what you wanted. You were so sure.'

I shrugged. I couldn't begin to explain to her how I felt.

51

The next few days were like the calm before the storm. I watched Eva grow stronger, younger. Thanis taught me how to control the power or, at least, how not to let it overwhelm me. She showed me a technique for closing a door within my mind that helped me regain a sense of normality. I felt the others were keeping away from me, leaving me alone for much of the day. I went for longer and longer solitary walks. I was amazed at the distances I could travel. I started to draw again and filled page after page. When I flipped through my sketchbooks I felt proud of my work. Despite myself, I began to accept the pact that I had made. I found myself thinking of the future, dreaming of the day my work would be displayed in some gallery.

One evening, early in October, I climbed down to the beach to watch the sun set. It was low tide. A thin film of water lay on the surface of the damp sand. I could see the sky and the gathering clouds reflected in it. I walked to the water's edge, my bare feet sinking into the cold sand. The wind was much stronger here. Angry waves were breaking just beyond the bay. I knew I would miss this place. Something would always draw me back here.

I was lost in my thoughts when I slowly became aware of voices. They were so muffled I couldn't make out what they were saying, but it sounded like singing. I looked around, no one was near. I scanned the clifftop. Still no one. There was only one place it could be coming from, the caves under Nuskhet's house.

I hesitated for a moment, remembering Thanis's injunction not to venture there alone. But I was one of them now. I'd nothing left to fear. I climbed easily up onto the rocks. I didn't need to worry about the seaweed that grew thicker the further out I went. I was as surefooted as a cat now. The sea was choppier here and full of shadows. Sometimes I was caught in the spray that cascaded over the side of the rocks. The tide was turning, struggling against itself as it began to surge back towards the shore.

I reached the entrance to the cave in a few minutes. My eyes adjusted quickly to the half light. I followed the worn path around the edge of the drop where the tide was beginning to rise. I wasn't worried about becoming trapped. I had plenty of time before high tide and, in any case, I was sure I could find the passage that led to Nuskhet's house.

I reached the stone steps I remembered from before and went up them cautiously. I entered the first of the tunnels. The voices were clearer here and I didn't want to be discovered. For a while I was walking in total darkness. My feet seemed to know where to land. I felt strangely excited, almost as if I knew I was about to make a discovery.

Unexpectedly the voices stopped. I waited for them to begin again but the silence was broken only by the distant booming of the incoming waves. I inched forward cautiously. I could feel cold air on my face although I was sure I wasn't near the surface yet. Suddenly I knew someone was there. I dropped back and waited. Soon I heard footsteps so faint they were almost imperceptible. A figure appeared from a side tunnel and hurried away into the darkness. I could only just make it out. Some instinct told me it was Thanis.

I waited, but no one else followed. The silence told me I was alone. I wanted to know what Thanis had been doing. Who had she been meeting? I entered the tunnel where she'd emerged. It twisted dramatically. I soon lost all sense of direction and didn't know if I was travelling inland or had turned back out to sea. My sense of smell let me down too. There was a trace of perfume in the air that disguised the natural odours of rock and sea.

I made another sharp turn and became aware of a flickering light ahead. I felt a strong surge of anticipation. Something was there. Something they'd been keeping secret. The chamber, when I arrived in it, took me completely by surprise. It was a small circular room formed naturally by some flaw in the rock.

As I approached I could see a semi-circle of glass saucers placed carefully on the floor. Each had a tiny flame that flickered back and forth in the draught. They were the source of the perfume I'd detected too, giving off a thin trail of fragrant smoke that rose into the darkness. When I got closer I could see there were symbols that looked like Ancient Egyptian hieroglyphs carved into the rock behind them. Beyond was an area of deep shadow my eyes could not penetrate.

I stooped down to pass through the low arch that formed the gateway to the secret room. My skin was tingling. I felt no fear at all. Something was drawing me into the room. Something that had drawn me from the beach and even drawn me into the cave that very first time I'd ventured there. I took a deep breath and looked around me. The room was alive with light and shadow. It played everywhere except for that one dark recess. I knew that was where I had to go. I picked up one of the lamps and headed into the darkness, ready to meet whatever waited there.

52

This was a darkness unlike that I had just left behind in the tunnels. It was so thick it was almost tangible. My eyes struggled to make out anything it was so absolute. The lamp's tiny flame diminished and quailed before it. I held it at eye level with one hand, and with the other searched in front of me.

I'd only walked a few steps when I found something. At first I thought I'd reached the back of the recess and was touching the wall. But as my fingers moved over the surface of the stone I discovered it curved too smoothly to be granite. It had a sort of warmth too, as though it still held the heat of a long distant sun. My fingers began to tingle. All my senses were alert. I put the lamp down intending to use both hands to work out the shape of whatever it was before me. The flame flared up briefly then extinguished itself. In that instant before the dark became absolute I saw it. A carved foot, tapering into finely curved claws.

I stepped back automatically. What had I touched? I was aware of something waiting there. I felt it watching me. I heard the slow beat of its heart. I could feel its breath. But it was stone. How could it be alive? I couldn't give up now. I knew this was something I had to see. I used the power as Thanis had taught me. I picked up the lamp and visualized it alight. It took me much longer than her, but at last there was a hint of blue light and the flame sprang back into life.

I walked forward boldly. I knew the statue, if that was what it was, was big. I held the lamp up, concentrating hard to maximize its light. Now I saw the row of symbols on the creature's chest. There was the Egyptian eye, the lotus, the scarab, and some other hieroglyphs I couldn't recognize.

As I moved the lamp higher I saw other symbols, strange letters from unknown alphabets, twisted shapes that culminated in the rune. I raised the light as high as I could and caught a glimpse of a gold face far above me.

'Now you know everything,' a voice rang out of the darkness. In my surprise I dropped the lamp and the sound of the breaking glass echoed all around me.

'Thanis?' I whispered. I saw something move and then a figure stepped forward out of the recess.

'Yes, look. Go ahead. This is what you came to see.' She lit two large torches that were held in loops of bronze attached to the walls at each side of the stone figure.

'I have been waiting for you,' Thanis continued. 'Yes, stare. She is beautiful, is she not? This is the Golden One, Sekhmet, the Devourer of Time. She is why we go on, why we do what we must to survive each age. We are her guardians and She guards us in return.'

'I . . . I recognize her,' I said softly. Before me towered the tall stone figure of the lion goddess I had struggled to draw that day in the museum. Only now her face was a golden mask which glowed warmly in the light of the torches.

'Of course you do,' Thanis said calmly. 'She called you that very first day in the museum. We had been waiting for you for a long time. My strength was failing. But I knew She would not fail us. Just as I knew you would discover our sanctuary eventually.'

'But you told me not to come here,' I said puzzled.

'Of course. You had to listen to your own voice, not mine. Now you are ready. The Ceremony can begin.'

53

As she finished speaking I became aware of the sound of rattles in the distance. Thanis signalled to me to be quiet. She walked over to the semicircle of lamps and passed her hands over each flame, whispering something as she did so. The flames grew strong, filling the chamber with their light. The statue of Sekhmet emerged from the dark recess clearly now. I guessed it was twelve feet tall. From where I stood it seemed to arise naturally from the rock, all apart from the carved symbols and the golden mask.

The sound of rattles was louder now. It was accompanied by people chanting and, occasionally, broken by a woman's voice singing. After a few minutes the procession entered the chamber where we waited. It was led by Nuskhet, holding his lion headed stick. Behind him the soloist, Kara, her two aunts Neret and Iaret, and finally Peter. Eva was nowhere to be seen. Each knelt by one of the lamps, leaving the central one free. Without anyone telling me, I knew that place was for me.

Thanis stepped into the centre of the semicircle. She was wearing a simple red dress that flowed over the floor around her feet. Her only ornament was the silver spiral which hung from a long chain around her neck. Directly behind her towered the lion goddess Sekhmet. The chanting gave way to a few moments of silence. As I listened I was sure once again that I could hear the statue breathing. I became aware of the waves filling the cave where I'd made my entrance. Then something else. Could it be rain falling far away on the surface?

Nuskhet banged on the ground with his stick and

everyone got to their feet. Thanis turned to the statue of the goddess and called out, 'Hear us, Mysterious One. Come to us, Golden One.

'Let your fires blaze brightly.

'Let your heat breathe life into us.'

As she spoke the waves seemed to get louder and closer so that it was impossible to separate her voice from theirs. I felt all the reality I knew slip away. I knew it was nothing. I could feel the ancient powers gathering around us. Feel their strength growing as inexorably as the tide rises with the moon.

'Welcome, Great One.'

Thanis took the spiral from her neck and pointed it at the ground. Immediately a circle of flames sprang up around her. They merged with the scarlet of her dress until she seemed to arise from a robe of fire.

'You who guard the gates of the horizon,
You alone hold the yesterday and the tomorrow.'

As I stared at the flames they seemed to rise higher and higher. The darkness receded. The small room was full of light. The gold face of the lion goddess shone like the sun. It was no longer a mask. It was alive with light. I could barely see Thanis. She'd become absorbed into the fire. She was fire.

'Hear us, Great Goddess. Imperishable One.
Hear us call you. Let your name be spoken.
Sekhmet, Devourer of Time.'

As Thanis called out the name the others fell to their knees and hid their faces. I alone stayed standing. I knew I had a part to play. I was prepared. I wouldn't fail them.

'Sekhmet, Devourer of Time,' I repeated softly. The name made my lips tremble.

'Hear the Gates of the Horizon close.
Time is no more.
There is no yesterday.
There is no tomorrow.
Beyond is Darkness.
Beyond is Chaos.
Let the stars tremble.
Let the earth weep.
Time is no more.

Imperishable One
You alone know no fear
Your voice is all powerful
Let your roar fill the sky.'

As she spoke I saw something I shall never forget. I saw the face of the goddess move. I saw those golden lips part. I saw the sharp feline fangs. I saw the chest rise and fall. I saw the stone breathe. A terrible roar resounded through the labyrinth of tunnels around us. I felt the earth tremble.

Thanis raised the spiral. I could see it spinning in the flames. Sparks of red light were shooting from it. I could see the silver consumed in the flames. Transformed. The spiral was light. Thanis held out her hand and gestured to me to join her inside the fiery circle. I stepped forward. My hand shook as I placed it in hers. I could feel the heat on my skin. It was like walking through a living curtain of flames. I felt the eyes of the goddess looking down on me. Cold, cruel eyes that knew no human feeling or compassion.

'Now,' Thanis whispered. 'Don't be afraid.' She handed me a small silver chisel and pointed to the row of symbols on the figure's chest. I knew immediately what my task was. I took the knife and at once my hand stopped shaking. This was my moment. I wouldn't fail.

Thanis stepped aside and I stood face to face with the goddess. I could see the carved symbols burning brightly.

The light was so strong I wanted to shield my eyes, but I knew I couldn't. There was no shield that could protect me from that terrible brightness. There was a space next to the rune and I knew I had to carve the spiral there.

My hand didn't falter. The chisel seemed to guide itself. The stone yielded to it. I knew I was the one. I was the one meant to inscribe the symbol in its proper place. I worked quickly. I understood now why they needed me. Without me there was no future. The power would leave them. Death would come in its place.

As I worked Kara began to sing. Her voice was so poignant that I turned my head around. The others had risen to their feet and were chanting again. Their voices merged with the sound of the waves, as if all of Nature was playing its part in the Ceremony. The lamps were flickering wildly as if in some sudden draught. I thought I saw Nuskhet glance anxiously at the darkness beyond the low archway, but I couldn't be sure. The flames that still separated me from them made everything waver.

I returned to my work. How easily the spiral emerged from the rock. The lines seemed to have a life of their own. They controlled the chisel. Guided it. I hadn't understood after all. I wasn't important. It wasn't my art, my work. I was only the vehicle. The servant. This thing that grew under my hand was so much more powerful than I could ever be.

I'd almost finished when I felt the wind rush into the room. The flames danced wildly. The chanting stopped suddenly. I looked up. Eva was stooping under the archway. Her pale hair was plastered to her forehead. Water streamed from her. She was out of breath and struggling for air. 'Is it over?' she gasped. 'Is it done?' She looked around at us, her eyes wild and staring. 'Listen, it's coming. Don't you know what's happening? There's a terrible storm. The tunnels are flooding. You have to leave. Hurry. It'll be high tide soon.'

139

'Not yet,' Thanis ordered. 'The sea won't harm us. The Ceremony must be finished.'

'It's too late. Let her leave,' Eva argued. 'Come here, Jessica. Hurry.'

I looked from one to the other, trying to understand what was going on.

'Don't worry. We are safe here.' Thanis turned her back on Eva and started the chant again. I raised the chisel. I only had to put the finishing touches to the spiral.

'Jessica,' Eva screamed my name. I turned intending to make her understand that I had to stay. That was when I saw the water creeping into the room.

'We are safe,' Thanis hissed at me. 'You must finish.'

I tried to obey, but I couldn't push the image of that dark, menacing water from my mind. The line wouldn't flow. The stone no longer yielded to my touch. I tensed. Something was wrong. I knew it.

'Jessica, come on. It's too late,' Eva pleaded. 'Leave them.'

I looked at Thanis. Her eyes shone angrily. 'Concentrate,' she ordered. 'You must.'

I don't know how I did it, but I did concentrate. I finished the spiral although every slight movement was a struggle. I felt the relief in the room. It was done.

Thanis carried on with the ceremony, her voice slow and even. The water had reached the recess where I stood. I felt it creep around my feet. I remembered her saying wind and waves couldn't hurt us. I only hoped that was true. The circle of fire still protected her. It seemed unaffected by the water.

'Sekhmet, Mysterious One
Open the Gates of the Horizon
Set free the yesterday
Set free the tomorrow
Let the spiral spin
Let the future come

Hear us, Powerful One
Protect us from the chaos
Let the solar eye shine upon us
Let us become as the imperishable stars
Let the spiral spin
Let the future come.'

As her voice faded a great roar filled the chamber. An icy wind rushed around us. My hair was blown across my face. My hand trembled. I felt the chisel slip from my fingers. 'No!' Thanis shouted loudly. I grabbed at it awkwardly, lost my balance and fell forward, putting my hand out to protect myself. The fierce light that had flowed around the goddess wavered and died.

'No!' Thanis shouted again. Her voice echoed round and round the room. 'What have you done? What have you done?'

I stared at her uncomprehending. I followed her eyes. The sudden change in the light made it hard to see. The small lamps were flickering so frantically. Shadows were dancing everywhere. What was she staring at?

'Is the Ceremony complete?' Nuskhet shouted.

I didn't hear Thanis's reply. I'd finally seen it. I saw what I'd done. For there, barely visible, running through the spiral, was a long scratch. The chisel must have caught it as I fell.

54

I looked on in horror. I couldn't move. The water was rising around my ankles. Cold and black and thick with the seaweed that had been swept along in its current. The lamps were all submerged. They floated slowly to the surface and turned erratically for a few moments before drifting away. Nuskhet began to speak, commanding the water to turn.

'Jessica, come on,' Eva shouted. Her voice was a lifeline. I had to get out of there. Time was running out. The water was reaching my knees. The current was pulling against my legs. It was hard to keep my balance. 'Hurry, there's no time to waste.' I looked at the others. They too seemed uncertain and confused. Only Thanis remained calm. She was still safe within the fiery circle.

A sudden surge of the cold black water swept into the room. I saw Nuskhet struggle then fall. His stick fell from his hand and was carried away with the current. I watched the golden lion's head disappearing into the darkness. Eva screamed as she was propelled forwards into the room. Peter fought his way across to her. The water was rising fast. Nuskhet was struggling to his feet, helped by his nieces and Kara.

Suddenly the light dimmed. The rising water had finally extinguished the flames around Thanis. I saw her dress clinging to her figure, the ruined skirts floating around her. The water was still rising unbelievably quickly. It had now reached the ends of her long hair. The only remaining light was the two torches set into the wall. The flames were dancing frantically and seemed in danger of being blown out at any minute. They threw their crazy reflections across the ruffled surface of the dark water.

Another surge of water flung me forward. I felt something wrap itself around my leg and drag me down. The water was dragging me away. I reached out in desperation for something to cling to. I think I grabbed hold of Thanis for I suddenly found myself being pulled back up to the surface. I gulped frantically at the damp, salt ridden air. There wasn't much of it. The water was so high that the archway was almost covered. All around me was chaos. If I didn't go now there would be no escape.

Eva was arguing with Peter. She saw me looking and started to make her way across to me. 'It's too late,' she said. 'You can't save them. Come on, can you swim?'

I nodded. I couldn't see how even swimming could help us now. Eva dived beneath the surface. I saw her head for the archway before she vanished in the murky waters. I was about to follow her when Thanis shouted something at me. Her words were lost in the roar of the wind and waves. It felt as if the whole Atlantic Ocean was trying to pour itself inside that small cave. I gazed at her helplessly. She walked calmly away from me. I saw her head for the recess where the goddess waited. Suddenly the torches went out. I was in absolute darkness.

There was barely any air. Time had run out. A final wave broke over my head. I gulped for air and let myself be carried down with the current. It threw me against the side of the archway and I feared I would be swept back into the room. Suddenly someone had hold of me. I felt them pull me through the archway and into the tunnel beyond.

55

Someone was holding me up. I coughed furiously, struggling to get some oxygen into my lungs. The noise was terrible. I couldn't see a thing. Then another wave broke over my head and I was swept away. I held my breath for as long as I could. I soon had to give up. I felt the salt water rushing into my throat. I knew I was drowning. I was aware of an intense cold paralysing my limbs. I managed to open my eyes but all around me was only the dark, murky water.

I had no idea where the current was carrying me, or even which way was up. I tried to swim but I no longer had any control over my body. I remembered, too late, the twists and turns that had led me to the secret room in the first place. The current threw me against the rock wall. I felt the shock of intense pain before I bounced off. The respite was brief. I was flung against the rock again. I wasn't going to survive. I lost consciousness.

The pain saved me. It brought me back to life. I struggled to regain consciousness. I realized I was no longer being flung around so drastically. The current was less strong here. Somehow I'd reached a larger tunnel alive. I knew this was my only chance. I forced my arms into action and began to swim. I went with the current, hoping it might carry me to higher ground. When my head emerged from the water I breathed as deeply as I could. Sometimes the tunnel roof would be only inches above me and I feared the worst. Then, just when it seemed hopeless, the water became more shallow. I felt its force weaken. I swam harder than ever, convinced I was within reach of dry land.

Eventually I realized I could walk. The water level was getting lower and lower. Soon it was just above my knees. I had no idea where I was, but I was sure that I'd travelled inland. I remembered that the tunnels went on for miles, leading to long-abandoned mines. There had to be a way out.

I lost all track of time. It seemed an age since I'd stood by the water's edge watching the sun set. Would I ever see that sun again? No, I mustn't let myself think like that. I mustn't think at all. All my thoughts were too terrible. I had to survive. I couldn't die now. Not alone in this awful darkness. In this endless maze of tunnels.

I'd almost given up hope when I glimpsed something in the distance. There was a faint glimmer of light. I found a new strength and broke into a run. I hurt everywhere but that didn't matter. There was light. It was getting stronger. There must be a way out. I longed to see the sky. To see blue after all this relentless black.

The air tasted sweet. I followed it to its source and found a narrow funnel that led up to the surface. I could barely make out the sky at the other end, but I didn't care. I could see freedom. Taste it.

It wasn't easy getting myself into that narrow funnel. The entrance was just out of my reach. Somehow I managed it. My eyes hadn't adjusted yet to the feeble light but I searched with my fingers tips until I felt a flaw in the granite. I managed to lodge one hand in the crevice and searched around frantically to find a foothold. My bare feet were too numb. Again and again they slipped back from the rock and I feared that I would never make it. I refused to give in. It was a miracle I was still alive. I couldn't die now when escape was within my reach.

The light was getting stronger when I finally managed to get a grip on the cold rock and heave myself up into the narrow funnel. I wedged myself in and took a few moments to rest. I could hear the water in the distance, its roar subdued now. I started to shiver. I had to get moving or my limbs would fail me. I worked my feet up a few inches at a time, then levered myself up above them. Sometimes I found a ledge my fingers could grip, at others I had to push my elbows into the side as hard as I could to stop myself from falling.

Once, when the surface was tantalizingly near, I did fall back a few feet. I screamed with frustration, then started the long slow haul back to the surface again. I used the pain to concentrate my mind. Nothing else existed except the certainty the surface was getting closer and that I would reach it.

56

I must have blacked out. When I came to I struggled to open my eyes. The sky was a deep blue, the sun still hot despite the cold wind. I was somewhere high up on the moors. Everything seemed so peaceful. The only sign of the storm that had passed were the puddles of water glistening through the bracken. I couldn't stand up. I crawled through the mud and water until I reached an old stone wall. I managed to pull myself to my feet and lean against it while I looked around. There was the sea in the distance. I recognized the headland and could just make out Nuskhet's house. It looked deceptively near.

I don't remember much of the journey I made back to the house. I was filled with a mixture of hope and dread. Hope that safety was ahead, rest and sleep, an end to this endless struggle. Dread of what I would discover there, of what might await. All that ended when I heard the voices calling my name. They were alive. Safe. Everything was going to be

OK. I shouted out as loudly as I could. I saw their figures appear, felt a warm blanket being wrapped around me, heard my name spoken gently, before I collapsed.

I slept for days. I was so feverish that I couldn't tell what was real, what was dream and what a nightmare. Shadowy figures moved around my room, familiar voices emerged from strange faces, night and day were all confused. Then one morning, suddenly, my head was clear. I remembered everything. I got up and made my way downstairs.

My legs were wobbly. The bruises had become a deep, mottled purple but the cuts had begun to heal. I could hear sound from somewhere at the side of the house and I made my way there. Nuskhet's servant was in the kitchen, busy baking. She stared at me and nodded. I sank into a chair, feeling helpless.

'I'll get the others,' she said brusquely.

The others. This was the moment I'd dreaded.

'Is everyone all right? They're all safe, aren't they?'

She looked at me coldly. 'I'll get the others,' she repeated.

She shuffled slowly out of the kitchen leaving me alone with my fears. I waited for ages but she didn't come back. I got up and tried to exercise my legs by walking back and forth across the room. I realized I was cut off from my past. No one knew where I was. Only Mel had known about Nuskhet, and she was dead. I had no idea what the future would bring. I'd failed everyone. I felt so useless.

It was getting dark when Eva arrived. She looked pale and tired but greeted me with a genuine warmth.

'We were all worried about you,' she said.

'I'm OK,' I told her. 'I thought you might blame me. You're all . . . safe?' I struggled over the word. Eva looked away. I watched her pale hair fall over her face and I knew.

'Who?' I whispered.

'Nuskhet. He was too weak to withstand the current. Kara. She tried to save him.'

'Neret and Iaret?'

'They're fine. They knew the way out.'

'And Peter?'

Eva nodded. 'He will be here soon. He found you on the moor. Don't you remember?'

I shook my head. There was only one name that had not been spoken. One name. It lay heavy in the air between us. I moved my lips but couldn't get the sound to come out.

'It wasn't your fault, Jessica. She chose to stay in the shrine. She couldn't face the future, not really.'

'But she wanted it. She wanted to live so badly,' I said quietly.

'The future will go on without her,' Eva said softly. 'Maybe it is better so.'

57

So here I am. Back in London, but not in my old room in Camden Town. I have my own flat in Chelsea now. A very expensive flat, three bedrooms, studio, a roof terrace where I like to stand at night and watch the stars. I'm a great success. Exhibitions in London, Bristol, Edinburgh. One coming up in New York. Everything, in fact, that Thanis promised. A whole new life.

Everything has changed, except for one thing. I still love to paint. I work every day. All day, and sometimes all night too. It's the only thing that gives me any peace of mind. A respite from the fears that plague me. I want my art to be perfect. You see, I have this horrible feeling that it was all my fault. That it wasn't the storm or the sudden flood that did it. It was me. I ruined the spiral. And that spoiled everything.

Eva says that's nonsense, but I know she's just trying to make me feel better. She often comes to keep me company, when she's well enough. She's my best friend now. Of course, I know lots of people, but I wouldn't call them friends. You see, it's not easy to make real friends, that's why I'm writing all this down. The things that have happened are like a great gulf between me and the rest of the world. I need to tell my story. To share my experiences. To find some peace of mind.

I'm always worried. I spend a lot of time looking in the mirror. I'm not vain. Far from it. I'm searching for lines around my eyes, wrinkles anywhere. I haven't found any yet. I'm not sure how I'd feel if I did find any. Would I be relieved or disappointed? No one wants to grow old. But does anyone really want to live for ever? The others are the same. You see, no one knows what will happen now. Was the Ceremony complete? Is the future safe? Or was it lost with the silver spiral?

If Thanis was here things would be different. She would know. We're all lost without her. Some of the others don't believe she's dead. They don't think she was human at all. They say no one knows where she came from. No one can remember when she first appeared. They pray she'll come back one day. In time for the next Ceremony.

I don't know what to believe. We never found her body, although we searched for days. We buried Nuskhet and Kara up on the moors, not far from the Wicca stones. We stayed there for weeks, searching, hoping, unable to accept what had happened. I still search for her everywhere. I see her on crowded streets, glimpse her disappearing through doorways, spot her through train windows. But I never find her.

Eva says I never will. I'm not so sure. You see, I did go back to the secret room. I had to see for myself. There was debris everywhere. The tunnels weren't easy to pass. In some places the roof had collapsed. In others great boulders had been thrown up by the sea. There were dead fish that stank, heaps of rotting seaweed, bits of old plastic bottles, rusting tin cans. I had to crawl to get into the chamber itself.

I was struck at once by a terrible chill in the air. I'd never felt such an icy cold before. I had to fight an impulse to flee. My torch swung round the room catching bits of broken glass in its beam. The air was stale and reeking. I remembered how the lamps had perfumed the air. The sense of loss was overpowering, but I had to go on. I raised my eyes from the floor. The two bronze torch holders were still anchored to the wall. Beyond them was darkness.

I aimed my torch into the recess. Its light faltered as if consumed by the hungry darkness. At first I could see nothing. Then, gradually, I made out the rows of hieroglyphs on the wall, their colours undimmed by the flood. Beyond them was rock. Bare, flat rock. I swung the torch back and forth across its rough, uneven planes. I could see the tiny crystals glimmering in the granite. I could see the beads of moisture clinging to the surface. But that was all. There was no trace of the statue I had felt with my own fingers. No trace of the golden mask. Just an awful emptiness. The goddess was gone.